HENRI-PIERRE ROCHÉ

*Jules et Jim*

*Introduction by Agnès Catherine Poirier*
*Afterword by François Truffaut*
*Translated by Patrick Evans*
*Afterword translated by Katherine C. Foster*

PENGUIN BOOKS

PENGUIN CLASSICS

Published by the Penguin Group
Penguin Books Ltd, 80 Strand, London WC2R ORL, England
Penguin Books (USA) Inc., 375 Hudson Street, New York, New York 10014, USA
Penguin Group (Canada), 90 Eglinton Avenue East, Suite 700, Toronto, Ontario, Canada M4P 2Y3
(a division of Pearson Penguin Canada Inc.)
Penguin Ireland, 25 St Stephen's Green, Dublin 2, Ireland (a division of Penguin Books Ltd)
Penguin Group (Australia), 250 Camberwell Road, Camberwell, Victoria 3124, Australia
(a division of Pearson Australia Group Pty Ltd)
Penguin Books India Pvt Ltd, 11 Community Centre, Panchsheel Park, New Delhi – 110 017, India
Penguin Group (NZ), 67 Apollo Drive, Rosedale, Auckland 0632, New Zealand
(a division of Pearson New Zealand Ltd)
Penguin Books (South Africa) (Pty) Ltd, 24 Sturdee Avenue, Rosebank, Johannesburg 2196, South Africa

Penguin Books Ltd, Registered Offices: 80 Strand, London WC2R ORL, England

www.penguin.com

First published in France by Editions Gallimard, Paris 1953
First published in Great Britain by Calder and Boyars Publishers Ltd, London 1963
Published in Penguin Classics 2011

009

This translation copyright © Marion Boyars Publishers 1963, 1993, 1998, 2006
Introduction copyright © Agnès Catherine Poirier, 2011
Afterword copyright © François Truffaut, 1980
Translation of main text © Patrick Evans, 1963
Translation of afterword © Katherine C. Foster, 1987, 1998, 2006
All rights reserved

The moral right of the translators and the authors of the introduction and afterword have been asserted

Set in 11.25/14 pt Dante MT Std
Typeset by Palimpsest Book Production Limited, Falkirk, Stirlingshire
Printed in Great Britain by Clays Ltd, St Ives plc

ISBN: 978-0-141-19463-9

www.greenpenguin.co.uk

# Contents

## Jules et Jim

Henri-Pierre Roché was born in Paris in 1879. After studying art at the Académie Julian, he became a journalist and art dealer, mixing with the avant-garde artistic set in Paris at the turn of the century. His friends and acquaintances included the artists Marcel Duchamp and Francis Picabia, and in 1905 he introduced Leo and Gertrude Stein to Pablo Picasso. In 1916, following his discharge from the French army, Roché went to New York and set up a Dadaist magazine, *The Blind Man*, with Duchamp and the artist Beatrice Wood. It wasn't until he was in his seventies that Roché wrote his semi-autobiographical first novel, *Jules et Jim*; his second novel, *Les deux anglaises et le continent*, was published in 1956. Roché died in 1959 in Sèvres, Hauts-de-Seine.

Agnès Catherine Poirier was educated at the Sorbonne, the Institut d'Etudes Politiques de Paris and the London School of Economics. She moved to London to write for *Le Monde*, and was subsequently UK arts correspondent for *Le Figaro* and political correspondent and film critic for *Libération*. She writes articles for the *Guardian*, the *Observer*, the *Evening Standard* and the *Independent on Sunday* and is a regular contributor to the BBC on politics and films. Her most recent book is *Touché! A French Woman's Take on the English* (2006).

François Truffaut was born in Paris in 1932 and developed a love of film at a young age, often playing truant from school to go to the cinema. In 1950, Truffaut joined the French army and was later arrested for attempting to desert. He then became a critic and editor of the film magazine *Cahiers du cinéma*, and made his first feature film *Les Quatre Cent Coups*, in 1959. Having stumbled across *Jules et Jim* in a secondhand book-stall, Truffaut befriended its author and in 1962 made the novel into a film. His *Jules et Jim*, which stars Jeanne Moreau, is today recognized as one of the seminal films of the French New Wave. In 1971 Truffaut made Roché's second novel, *Les deux anglaises et le continent*, into a film. He died in 1984.

# Introduction

'It was about the year 1907.' So starts Henri-Pierre Roché's *Jules et Jim*. Was there ever a better year than 1907 to be young and in Paris?

Henri-Pierre Roché is Jim, a Parisian – though one has to pronounce his name the English way, 'Djim not Zheem'. Jules is his best friend, in real life Franz Hessel, Proust's first translator into German. Both men are in their twenties. At this particular time in her long history, Paris is the city of eternal youth. The world's youngsters flock to the French capital to grab a share of its carefree gaiety, and they, in exchange, contribute to the city's radiance. 'The new Athena', 'The new Babylon', 'the new Jerusalem' as *flâneurs* can see written in big bold red letters above the new theatres and cabarets of Pigalle. Paris is the capital of all capitals, the incubator of avant-garde, the laboratory of new ideas, and, of course, the garden of forbidden fruits.

Henri-Pierre Roché was approaching seventy-four when he wrote *Jules et Jim*, his first novel. A recollection of his youth and of his amours, *Jules et Jim* is written in a style reminiscent of Debussy and Ravel: furiously modern, fast, fresh and free. Once young in Paris, forever young? No doubt.

In 1907, Henri-Pierre Roché is an inquisitive young man, curious about the world, eager to discover new horizons in life, whether the cleavage of a new lady friend or the curve of a cello in a Braque collage. An avid art collector, a discoverer of new talents, he makes friends wherever he goes. In Paris, he introduces

Picasso to Gertrude Stein, in New York he lives with Marcel Duchamp and their mistress and fellow artist Beatrice Wood. Henri-Pierre Roché is the archetype of the French intellectual dilettante. Albert Sorel, his professor at Sciences-Po, the Institute of Political Sciences of Paris, once tells him: 'Give up diplomacy. Be an inquiring mind. It's not a job yet. It soon will be. The French have shut themselves away behind their frontiers for far too long. They should travel. You will always find some newspapers which will pay for your escapades.' Advice Roché is going to apply to the letter.

Where else to start his travelling but in Paris, the most cosmopolitan of all cities where the world's nationalities are represented in its every *quartier*? Roché and his friends are true Europeans, fluent in at least four languages. For them, chauvinism is an alien concept. How could they see the clouds looming on the horizon? They have only one homeland, the European culture. Their *patrie* is that of Goethe, Baudelaire, Strindberg, Apollinaire, Shakespeare.

Did Henri-Pierre Roché and Franz Hessel, our Jules et Jim, meet with the then twenty-six-year-old Austrian Stefan Zweig who, at about the same time, as he writes in *The World of Yesterday*, promised himself Paris as a gift for the first year of his freedom? Zweig too felt the elation of the time:

> And nowhere could you ever have experienced the artless yet wonderfully wise lightness of life more happily than in Paris, where it was gloriously affirmed in the city's beauty of form, mild climate, wealth and traditions. [. . .] We were under no compulsion, we could speak, think, laugh and criticise as we liked [. . .] the street was common property! [. . .] You walked, talked, and slept with whoever you liked, regardless of what anyone else thought. [. . .] Paris accommodated everyone side by side; here was no above and below, [. . .] there was always laughter in the air somewhere, or the sound of someone calling out in friendly tones. [. . .] Nothing was stiffly formal. It was easy to meet women and

easy to part with them again [. . .] What a carefree life that was!
You could live well in Paris, especially when you were young!

Did Jules and Jim meet twenty-three-year-old German Daniel-
Henry Kahnweiller, son of a banker and father of all art dealers,
who would, in the spring of 1907, climb up the stairs of the
decrepit Bateau Lavoir studio in Montmartre and find the young
black-haired Pablo Picasso standing silent and perplexed in front
of his *Demoiselles d'Avignon*? Paris, 1907: the place and time Jules
and Jim live in, one of continuous experiment and limitless possibilities, where one can be free, creative and, it seems, always
merry. *Jules et Jim* is an epoch; it is also a quest. That of harmonious love, kind, free, selfless and passionate, a pioneering love
which keeps reinventing itself. Jules and Jim find the freedom
they seek in the arms of many passing lovely ladies, the mysteri-
ous Lucie, the extravagant Odile, the placid Gilberte, the simple
Michèle, but they find love in only one woman, Kate.

Who is Kate? She is the woman with the archaic smile. The
same smile Jules and Jim saw once on the lips of an excavated
sculpture, which they travelled to see at an open-air museum on
the Adriatic. 'They lingered round the goddess in silence, gazing
at her from different angles. Her smile was a floating presence,
powerful, youthful, thirsty for kisses and perhaps for blood.'
There, they decided that, if they ever saw a woman with such a
smile, they would both follow it. Kate is not only a smile, though,
she's a force. 'She is Napoleon,' says Jim to Jules. Cruel? No, free.
In this love triangle, all parties are free and equal, always loyal to
one another; this is what makes it so subversive.

Kate may be the epitome of female beauty, but she behaves in
what many would consider a masculine way. 'Her gospel was that
the world was rich and that you could cheat a bit sometimes; she
always asked God's forgiveness in advance and was confident she'd
get it.' Kate had been drawn by Jules's mind but she also needed a

male of her own sort, Jim. What about Jules? Unable to truly satisfy Kate, he chooses to give her away to Jim, thus making sure of never losing her. From her husband, he becomes her confidant, agreeing to divorce and let Jim marry her. What about Jim? Jim takes her, loves her, wants to marry her and have children with her. However, it is not that simple. Even the purest love can be contrarian.

Jules loves Kate, Jim loves Kate, Kate loves Jules and Jim, yet all are independent. 'They are alone and together,' writes Henri-Pierre Roché. It would be wrong to view Kate's independence as a political manifesto. She is no more an activist than Jules and Jim are. She doesn't fight for a cause nor does she take refuge behind a group. Activism is only a way of escaping personal responsibility. Kate is her own pioneer.

Of course, we would probably not know about Henri-Pierre Roché and his *Jules et Jim* if it hadn't been for the enlightened enthusiasm of a reader of his, the twenty-three-year-old François Truffaut. A budding film critic in 1955, Truffaut, like Roché an eternal *amoureux*, is immediately struck by this story of a tender love triangle ruled by 'a new aesthetic moral ethic which is constantly under review'.

François Truffaut feels so attracted to *Jules et Jim*'s story that he swears he'll make it into a film. In 1962, three years after Henri-Pierre Roché's death, *Jules et Jim* is released internationally: a resounding success both with the critics and the public. *Jules et Jim* is the blueprint for Truffaut's entire oeuvre. Film after film, François Truffaut will never cease to try and answer those questions: How to live and love? How to love and be free within a couple? How to be free and not cruel to others? In *Jules et Jim*, the quest for free and harmonious love is almost found. There is no competition between Jules and Jim in their love for women in general and the magnificent Kate in particular. What only counts for the three of them is *la joie de vivre*.

It is today impossible to think of Jules, Jim and Kate and not see Jeanne Moreau who plays Kate, or Catherine in the film, wearing a black and white Breton top, cycling away, her hair in the wind, the men in her life in hot pursuit.

In June 2000, commenting on the film she saw for the first time in thirty years, Jeanne Moreau said:

*it is the dreamed image of amorous life. However, today, many would be quick to call their relationship a perverse ménage-à-trois. Truth is, it is not a ménage-à-trois but an equal double love story. The characters all remain individuals. None is consumed in a fusional passion; none is lost in the other. Their individual integrity remains intact. This is what is difficult to understand today and what makes their love story so revolutionary.*

François Truffaut wanted to celebrate Henri-Pierre Roché's *Jules et Jim*, be as faithful as possible to the book and even more importantly to its style. 'It is about avoiding clichés,' the young director declared just after the film's release. The tacit intimacy which reigned on the shoot meant that Truffaut could translate in images *Jules et Jim*'s constant jubilation. 'We were perfectly in synch. The film is *un moment arrêté*, a fixed impression. You can almost touch the intensity and fluidity of life. We were not acting, just being ourselves. It was such a joyous time. Light and grave,' says Jeanne Moreau.

The gravity of *Jules et Jim* comes from the fact that it follows characters from their late twenties to their late thirties. Adult youth, much more profound than adolescent youth, always carries an edge. Their feelings cut deeper.

*Jules et Jim* depicts an excess of life, rather than life in excess. Their love story is neither neurotic nor muddled nor even bitter. It is rooted in desire and a never-ending curiosity, kindness and respect too. Jules, Jim and Kate delve into the nature of love: an instant that is so difficult to make last.

Agnès Catherine Poirier, 2011

# PART I

## *Jules et Jim*

I

## Jules and Jim

It was about the year 1907.

Jules, short and plump, a stranger to Paris, had asked Jim, tall and thin, whom he hardly knew, to get him into the *Bal des Quat-z'Arts*, and Jim had found him a ticket and taken him to the costumier's. It was while Jules was gently turning over one material after another and choosing a simple costume, that of a slave, that Jim's friendship for Jules was born. The friendship grew during the ball, which Jules took in serenely, his eyes round with wonder and brimming with humour and tenderness.

The next day, they had their first real conversation. Jules had no woman in his life in Paris, and he wanted one. Jim had several. He introduced Jules to a young musician. At first things looked promising. For a week Jules was rather taken, and so was she. Then Jules decided that she was too cerebral; and she, that he was too placid and ironical.

Jules and Jim saw each other every day. They sat up late at night, each teaching the other the language and literature of his own country. They showed each other one another's poems and translated them together. Their talk was leisurely; neither had ever found so attentive a listener. The regulars at the bar soon concluded, without the two young men's realizing it, that their relationship must be abnormal.

Jim introduced Jules into literary cafés frequented by celebrities. Jules was appreciated there and Jim was pleased. In one of these

3

cafés Jim had a girlfriend, a pretty, independent, casual young woman who could stand the nocturnal pace in Les Halles better than all the poets and still be on her feet at six in the morning. Loftily, as if from a height, she distributed her brief favours; and whatever life might do to her she kept her outlaw liberty and an immediate wit that always found its mark. The three of them went out together several times. She disconcerted Jules, whom she considered nice, but ineffective. He thought her remarkable but alarming. She brought along a pleasant silly girl for Jules – and Jules found her pleasant, but silly.

So Jim couldn't do anything for Jules. He persuaded him to go hunting on his own, but Jules, possibly through being bothered by his still imperfect French, never got anywhere. Jim told Jules, 'It's not a question of language,' and gave him a lecture on strategy.

'You might just as well lend me your shoes or your boxing-gloves,' said Jules, 'all your things are too big for me.'

Jules, against Jim's advice, had recourse to professionals. But there was no satisfaction in that.

They fell back on their translations and conversations.

## 2

## Jim in Munich

At this juncture Jules's mother, getting on in years but still full of life, arrived from Central Europe to see her son in Paris; an anxious time for Jules. She went through all his linen to make sure there wasn't a button missing anywhere. She took Jules and Jim out to dinner in the best restaurants, but she wanted both of them to be in frock-coats and top hats. Jules found this a strain. Eventually she left.

One rainy evening three months later, Jules improvised a dinner for Jim and himself in his two furnished rooms. Jim, happening to open the fireplace of the tiled stove, found Jules's top hat sitting in it, without any wrapping and covered with a delicate layer of soot. Jules said with satisfaction, 'You see, if I keep it there it's out of the way and the soot protects it against the moth.' To which Jim answered, 'I'm not your mother, Jules.'

They used to have their meals in little wineshops. Cigars were their only extravagance; each picked out the best cigar for the other. They frequented the Concert Mayol and the Gaîté-Montparnasse, where Colette was miming.

Jules told Jim at length about his home district and the girls there. He loved one of them, Lucie, whose hand he had asked – in vain, which was the reason for his departure to Paris. Now, after six months, he was going back to see her.

'There's another one, too,' said Jules; 'Gertrude. She leads her own life and she's got a fine little boy. She understands my nature. And she doesn't take me seriously. Here she is.'

Jules took a photo of Gertrude out of his wallet. She was lying naked on a beach, girdled only by an incoming wavelet, while her year-old son sat on his mother's buttocks and faced the open sea, like an infant Eros on a fortified citadel.

'And there's one more, Lina; I might be in love with her if I wasn't in love with Lucie. Look, she's something like this.' And with small, slow strokes of his pencil on the round marble table he sketched a face.

Jim, talking away, glanced at this face; then he said to Jules, 'I'm coming with you.'

'To see them?'

'Yes.'

'Bravo!' said Jules.

Jim wanted to buy the table, but the owner of the bar wouldn't sell unless he bought all the twelve tables in the place.

# 3

## *Three Beauties*

To prepare the way, Jules set out a week in advance for Munich, where he had spent two years in and around these three women's company.

He rented two large rooms for Jim in the house of respectable people, and announced Jim to his three friends, with such a different description in each case that they found themselves at sea when they compared notes.

As soon as Jim arrived Jules introduced him to Lina, who knew the story of the table.

To Jules's surprise, Lina (a beautiful young poppet with a teasing wit) and Jim, even before they had finished the cakes they were taking with their tea, saw eye to eye on the following points:

(a) There wasn't much likeness between Jim and the description of him which Jules had given her.

(b) There was almost no likeness between Lina and the drawing on the table.

(c) They got on very well together but, to save Jules's time and their own, issued a joint bulletin that the expected grand passion would not be forthcoming.

'What clear, quick reactions!' said Jules. 'I do envy you . . .'

As for Lucie and Gertrude, Jules revealed them both at once to Jim, at a supper in the city's most modern bar.

Once their evening coats had fallen away the two women

blossomed out in striking contrast. They sat down at a pale wooden table which was quickly spread with a cloth and strange glasses.

A shy, happy smile played over Jules's lips, telling the other three that he held them in his heart.

Leisure, without constraint, enfolded them all.

'How on earth have you managed,' said Jim, thinking aloud, 'to bring together at one and the same time two women who are so different and so—' He didn't finish his sentence; silence uttered on his behalf the word *beautiful*. The women heard it.

Jules flushed with pleasure. He was about to reply, but Gertrude checked him with up-raised hand and said, 'Jules is our confidant; and our producer, too. He's got a fertile imagination and the patience of an angel. He puts us into his novels. He consoles us, he teases us; he pays court to us, but he doesn't try to monopolize us. He only forgets one thing – and that's himself.'

'What lovely praise!' said Jim.

'So when he calls us we come,' said Lucie, tilting her head slightly back.

Jules, in his own comic way, told them how his plan for Lina and Jim had fallen through. Lina had already told them herself by telephone.

'But of course,' said Gertrude. 'Lina and Monsieur Jim aren't right for one another. Lina's a spoilt child, and Monsieur Jim doesn't like that.'

'What does he like?' asked Jules.

'We shall see,' said Lucie impassively.

For the second time the gravity of her voice made its impact on Jim. To find himself sitting between these two women made him almost ill at ease, he would have liked to spend the whole time looking at each of them.

It seemed like the start of a dream.

It was not long before Jules, a master of ceremonies, proposed that they abolish once and for all the formalities of *Monsieur* and *Mademoiselle* and *Madame* by drinking to brotherhood, *Brüder-schaft trinken*, in his favourite wine, and that to avoid the traditional and too obtrusive gesture of linking arms the drinkers should touch feet under the table – which they did. Carried away by his happiness Jules quickly withdrew his own feet.

Jim's stayed for a moment between one foot of Gertrude's and one of Lucie's. Lucie was the first gently to withdraw her foot.

She was a long-skulled, Gothic beauty; she took her time over everything she did, so that other people found every moment endowed with the same abundant value as she conferred on it herself. Her nose, mouth, chin and forehead expressed all the pride of a German province, the allegorical role of which she had once played as a child in a religious festival. She came of an upper-middle-class family and was studying painting.

Gertrude was thirty; her beauty was classical Greek and she was a born athlete. She won ski races without training, and she could jump off a tram going full tilt and stop dead without an effort as she landed. She made you want to get to know her muscles. She had a fatherless son, aged four years; she didn't believe in fathers. She lived by her art as an illuminator, so she had her ups and downs. She was nobly born; she was under a boycott from her caste, but the artists respected and cherished her.

The evening flowed on like a winding river. They were all on the top of their form and sparks began to fly. One thing they had in common: they were comparatively indifferent to money and felt they were pawns in God's fingers; though Gertrude would have said that God was the Devil.

Jules was talking very well. But towards two in the morning he began being a bit too much of an expert about human souls and situations, and tried to counterbalance this by putting in a risky joke here and there. This might have been compensation – saying in public what he didn't dare to do in private. He poked fun at the two girls and himself and came near to poking it at Jim too; after all, hadn't he admitted them into a paradise whose gates he could never be sure of entering himself? He may have been feeling, prophetically, that this was how things were. His paean of homage and delight began to be punctuated with scratches, little lunges with the claws out, and there was an embarrassing passage in which he undertook to tell the Creator, lengthily, how to shatter the creation to bits and remould it nearer to the heart's desire.

Something obvious was dawning – namely, that while Jules was a delicious friend he hadn't got the stuffing to make a satisfactory husband or lover. He suspected it himself, as he had done before, and tried to drown the suspicion in a flood of words.

'He's wrecking his evening, he always does,' said Gertrude regretfully, when Jules had got up for a moment to go off after the cigarette-girl. Lucie shook her head indulgently.

Jules monopolized their final quarter of an hour with his ramblings; he bungled his effects, repeated them, and wouldn't let the others get a word in edgeways. All three were suffering on his behalf, and at the same time beginning to want to see each other again – without Jules.

Jim was seeing this side of Jules for the first time. On second thoughts he realized that there had been traces of it in their talks, when Jules, without the real presence, the sacrament of beauty, was borne away on the wings of his own eloquence.

'What an amazing night we've had!' said Jim. 'Two flowers, those girls, and so different; sacred love, profane love . . . I don't really want to see them both at the same time again.'

'I know what you mean. Which one struck you most?'

'I'm still dazzled,' said Jim, 'I'm in no hurry to find out. What about you?'

'I've asked Lucie to marry me and I shall ask her again. Gertrude consoled me when Lucie turned me down. I took Gertrude and her son away, to Italy, to the sea. She gave me her body but not her love . . . Look, Jim, when I met Lucie I was scared. I didn't want my feelings to run away with me. We were touring in the mountains; she had hurt her foot, and she allowed me to look after her; I used to change the dressings. I'd have been glad if her foot had never got better.'

'I've been getting to know her hand,' said Jim.

'It was I who didn't get better,' Jules went on. 'When she was all right again I took my courage in both hands and proposed. She said *No* – but so sweetly that I'm still hoping.'

# 4

## *Gertrude*

Jim was an obstacle between Lucie and Jules.

At the end of a fortnight, after a siege which she made heroic and amusing, Gertrude gave herself to Jim. She came to see him in the evening once or twice every week. She was a generous, full-blooded creature. When they were not making love she told him all about her own life, which she looked upon as a perpetual game against God; she was always the loser. A whole gamut of Northern temperament and emotions, such as he had never met before, was revealed to Jim. She told him about her problems. Neither of them slept when they were together, though Jim did sometimes feel his eyelids flicker. She liked his way of listening but never gave him her close attention. She was fascinated by Napoleon; her daydream was that she'd meet him in a lift one day and he'd give her a child, and after that she'd never see him again.

'Our Jules is a charming man,' she said. 'He understands women better than any man I know, and yet, when it comes to taking us – he loves us too much and not enough. Sometimes he's witty, sometimes he wants us; either way he always chooses the wrong moment. I've done my best to help him but it's no good. He turns Lucie into a patient idol and worships her. Jules is a discoverer and a poet, but as a husband he'd be too gentle, one would always be in his debt.'

Gertrude and Jim usually finished their nights together by

walking in the woods at sunrise. They took a hired carriage to fetch the handsome four-year-old, who sat on the box beside the old driver and learnt to hold the reins and put the horses to a gallop, cracking the whip and swearing, his fair hair ruffling in the wind.

Then Jim went back to spend the day sleeping and musing on the things Gertrude had told him.

Jules was kept informed by both of them. He saw as much of them as before, but not together. With each of them he talked of the other, and, as was his habit, drew a satisfaction of his own from their pleasures.

## 5

### Jules and Lucie

Jules arranged a romantic excursion in the woods with Lucie and Jim. He made up a fairy-story: Lucie was the fairy, holding Jules by one hand and Jim by the other; a childish and charming picture – Jim's hand loved Lucie's. They found this sudden familiarity embarrassing. Jules was relaxed and expansive and didn't have his usual rush of words.

Jim got a small parcel and was surprised when he recognized the elegant handwriting of the address. Inside was a note from Lucie: 'I should like to see you alone. Can you come to my flat tomorrow evening, about ten? This is the key of the main door.'

It was the custom in this city to shut the big front door at ten o'clock in the evening; every tenant had his own key.

Jim, who was early for once, walked up and down. He was holding the key in his pocket and thinking of Lucie and Jules.

Lucie's little drawing-room was enhanced by a fresco in quiet colours, painted by herself. She received him simply. 'We've never had an opportunity of meeting without Jules,' she said. 'I want to talk to you about him. You and he are friends and I want your support. He's about to visit the town where my home is, and he hopes I'm going to let him ask my father for permission to marry me. But I shan't let him. I should be glad if I felt you were near him then . . . But he hardly dares ask you to come with him.'

'Why?' said Jim.

'Because – because of Gertrude,' she said.

'I'll be there,' said Jim.

She served tea. The things about her, all carefully chosen, and her voice and gestures, reflected a deep underlying calm, a meditative atmosphere, a tradition of duty and acceptance. Jim realized how badly Jules needed Lucie, quite apart from her beauty. She would never marry him. Was she trying to spare Jules as much pain as she could?

They talked about Jules; and also about his poems, several of which Lucie had just copied out for him and still had with her. Her manuscripts were incomparably fine. It was only when his poems had emerged in this form that Jules felt they had really been born into the world. Lucie's handwriting, unhurried and unretouched, apparently effortless yet without blemish, moved straight towards its objective over the tiny pits and hollows of the sepia paper.

Jim was envious of Jules when she read out one of the poems, in a voice as fine as her calligraphy. Nothing she did was below her own standard.

Why had Jules led him to this shrine?

Jim asked Lucie to show him her paintings; which she did. They were temperate and harmonious.

He was finding it impossible to go; but midnight came, and he took his leave with a feeling of reverence towards her.


Lucie went home to her family. Gertrude went to the country, with her son and a lover.

# 6

## *Lucie and Jim*

A week later Jules and Jim were alone in a carriage in the little local train bearing them towards Lucie. The journey took six hours. Jules, though leisurely in speech and manner as usual, was agitated. He told Jim a dream which he had had that night.

'You and I were picking our way cautiously along the tops of the walls of a tall house which was being demolished. If we had fallen off we should have gone into some brambles. You were in front and I was following, holding Lucie's hand behind my back. Further behind there were Gertrude and some other people. You got to the end of the wall and couldn't go any further. As soon as we stopped I felt giddy. I wondered if you were going to turn round. Suddenly you jumped, just like when you're pole-vaulting, only you hadn't got your pole. People shouted, but you were already standing up smiling on the opposite wall, six yards away. Then I woke up.'

Jules went on without a break, 'Shall we play dominoes?'

'Yes,' said Jim, who didn't like the game.

From his bag Jules took a set of extra-thin dominoes which his mother had given him, and they played for a long time. Jim did his best but Jules kept on winning. There were still two hours to go, and Jules began telling the story of Lucie and himself from the beginning: her love for another man and the unhappiness and illness it had brought to her, and then how he himself had looked after her and had gradually begun hoping that he stood a chance. Jim realized how powerful this love was, and it upset him.

Jules devoted their first day in the little town to a pilgrimage which made a complete though distant circuit round Lucie's home. He had seen the house only once before, for a few hours on a winter evening. What he wanted was to catch sight of Lucie reading at her window (which she probably never did) and to gaze at her from far off before going to the house itself. They walked up steep alleyways between high garden-walls and had tea out of doors under an arbour, huddling and hiding so as not to be seen by Lucie, and peering at a house which they soon discovered to be the wrong one. In this waking dream Jules went a bit wild, the house was a mirage, it was everywhere; they walked and walked, out of their depth.

On the next day they found it just where it ought to be – at the end of a level drive, a huge white house surrounded by its own park. Jim was introduced to a halo of white hair, Lucie's father, old but still with plenty to say. Lucie kept in the background when her father was there. Order and precision reigned.

Lucie had booked two large rooms for Jules and Jim in an inn built of pine-logs, outside the town; it was prettily situated on a hill; you could see the house from there, and with binoculars it was even possible to exchange signals.

In this setting which she had chosen they waited for chances of seeing her. They would have gone to the house every day, but they had to take care of her parents' susceptibilities and avoid giving the little town too much to gossip about.

They were often invited. Jim was a success on the tennis court in the park but less so in the drawing-room, where he was bored. It was the other way round with Jules, who was determined to charm the father at least, and others too if he could. The house was spacious, full of elder sisters, nephews, nieces, servants and pedigree dogs.

They had come for six days, they stayed six weeks. Jules was in a state of troubled ecstasy and couldn't bring himself to put his question; Lucie gave him no encouragement – and how lovely it all was!

Lucie's younger brother, a lively, perceptive student, arrived and the four of them began making day-long outings together, with rucksacks, in the wooded hills. Occasionally Jules would find himself alone with Lucie; and occasionally the same thing happened to Jim.

Was it the continual presence of Jules's love? Was it the influence of this gentle family life, with its provincial ritual which made such a perfect setting for Lucie? Or was it – just Lucie herself? Jim, in spite of himself, gradually fell in love with her. Jules, unconsciously, helped him; so did the brother, consciously; and perhaps Lucie helped too.

One day Lucie, as she walked beside Jim through the forest, paused to adjust the laces of her supple leather boots, watched Jules and her brother enter an inn some way further on, and said to Jim: 'Let's sit down. We've got time. Tell me what you're thinking about.'

'It's like this,' said Jim. 'Really, Jules is happy, in his own way, and just wants things to go on. He's seeing you often, in idyllic circumstances, and he's living on hope.'

'Would you be glad if I married him?'

'For his sake, yes, but not for yours.'

'And not even for his sake. If I was married to him I should turn into a shrew. I admire his work, and he's kind and charming, but I can't help feeling cross at his being determined to marry me.

'Jim, I got hurt too, before I ever met Jules. Badly. I expect he's told you. It hurts me to watch him getting hurt. You're his friend. Help me to help him, will you? Or just help me.'

She placed her slender, trembling hands in his. A round tear was brimming in each of her eyes. Without a word Jim took her in his long arms and lifted her up; it was almost a shock to discover how light her body was. He carried her over to a fallen tree-trunk, sat down and put her on his knees. They didn't talk. He was looking at her face from very close to; he tried to think of Jules, but he could feel Lucie's hair brushing against his lips.

'Do you still love him?' said Jim.

'Who?'

'The first one.'

'Perhaps . . . But it's fading into the distance now, and it's got to fade right out. What about you, Jim?'

'Me?'

'You've been in love, Jim. Really in love, Jim; I can feel you have. Why didn't you marry her?'

'Things didn't turn out that way.'

'Where is she now?'

'In France.'

'What's she like?'

'Chaste. Like you.'

Jim felt the pressure of Lucie's arm.

'D'you still love her, and does she still love you?'

'Yes, but we don't see each other often, although we're both free.'

'Don't cause unhappiness, Jim . . .'

'And now there's something new.'

'What is it?'

'I admire you, Lucie. I'm getting to know you, I love seeing you. I'm afraid of forgetting Jules.'

'We mustn't forget Jules, we must head him off.'

They were silent again. She quoted a poem:

*Alle das Neigen*
*von Herzen zu Herzen*
*ach wie so eigen*
*schaffet das Schmerzen*

'Translate,' she said.

*'All the liking from heart to heart and back again*
*Ah Lord, dear Lord, how it doth fashion pain!'*

– said Jim.

'Not bad,' she said, smiling, 'though you did put in "Ah Lord, dear Lord!" which wasn't there before. What about Gertrude?' she asked suddenly.

'Gertrude? . . . Just wonderful fun,' said Jim.

Jim had nipped in his lips one of Lucie's curls; the wind had sent it straying over his mouth. She bent her long neck and, through her hair, gave him her lips.

She got up gently. They rejoined the others.

Other walks followed. Jim's heart felt too big for his chest. The colour came back into Lucie's cheeks and gaiety into her ways.

Summer veered quickly towards autumn. Jules proposed to Lucie, adding that whatever her answer might be he would always be at her mercy. Lucie replied that though her heart was touched she would probably never feel able to marry him, and that she hoped the close friendship between them would nevertheless remain undiminished.

Jules turned white, though he had been expecting this; he kissed her hands and sought out Jim.

'Jim,' he said, 'Lucie won't have me. I'm terrified of losing her, I can't bear to let her go out of my life. Jim – love her, marry her, and let me go on seeing her. What I mean is, if you love her, stop thinking that I'm always in your way.'

Jim said, 'This is how things are with Lucie and me,' and told him the day-by-day story of their relationship.

To his surprise and pleasure Jules's face cleared. Jules said, 'The last time you played tennis with Lucie, against her brother and cousin, you looked as if you belonged together.'

Jules went off to find Lucie, and told her, 'Jim has been talking to me'; he complimented her tactfully and offered himself as a protector for her and Jim. She said, 'Our affection has only just been born, it must be left undisturbed, like a new-born baby.'

One evening Jules told them, 'I'll tell you about my suicide.' They were on the *qui vive* at once, for this was a side of Jules that they were afraid of.

This was his story: 'I was fifteen. I made up my mind to die. I put a spirit-stove under my bed, on a pile of books; my funeral pyre! I lit the stove. I lay down on my bed and made myself comfortable, then with two quick cuts with my razor I severed the veins in both wrists.' He showed them the white lines of the scars. 'The blood gushed out, very fast at first, and then stopped. I lost consciousness. When I came to myself my mother was at my bedside, there were bandages on my wrists and the doctor was there. The bed hadn't caught fire properly, but there had been enough smoke for the cook to see it coming out at the top of the door, which they had forced open.'

'What did your mother say?'

'She never said a word about it.'

'That was wise of her,' said Jim. 'How many storeys were there in the building?'

'Six,' said Jules.

'A nice tall pyre,' said Jim.

'Jules,' said Lucie, 'you were sacrificing your life for some ideal of your own, of course. But what about any little children on the upper floors? You might have burnt them to death.'

Jules was troubled: 'Good heavens!' he said, 'I never thought of that.'

Another time he told them: 'I was ten. On our way to school we had to cross a small waste lot where there was an embankment of yellow earth. All the boys liked crossing by this embankment. On it one day, Hermann, who was a friend of mine, snatched my satchel and threw it on the ground and punched me on the nose; he said I was a dirty Jew. My nose bled and I didn't understand, but that evening my mother explained to me.

'Hermann often attacked me there but never anywhere else; it was like a ritual. I could have made a slight detour and avoided the embankment, but I never did. Besides, I liked Hermann, really.'

'For his own sake?' said Jim. 'Or because he hit you?'

'Both,' said Jules.

Jules said to Lucie: 'Jim isn't very intelligent.' Lucie's eyebrows went up. 'He doesn't need to be.' Her eyebrows came down again. 'He's like a hound that simply follows the scent.' Lucie smiled. 'He crumples his nose up, looking for his fleas,' Jules went on, carried away by the comparison. They laughed simultaneously.

'He looks into your eyes for a moment,' she said, 'then he puts his front paws on your shoulders and licks your face and you fall over! . . . He turns round and round before lying down. It'll be years before he gets himself settled.'

'Would you wait for him, perhaps?' said Jules.

'Who knows?' said Lucie. 'Anyway, he's helping me to start living again.'

On their last evening Lucie promised to come and see them in Paris next spring.

'Forgive me, both of you,' said Jules, 'for going on hoping. My love is for always – that's how it feels to me. I don't have to hurry.

I should like Lucie to be ill and deserted and disfigured, so that I could rescue her and devote my life to her.'

'All of which may yet happen,' said Lucie, with a colourless smile.

In the train, Jim explained to Jules that Lucie and he didn't feel they were ready for marriage. Was she really cut out to have a husband and children? He was afraid she would never find happiness on this earth. He thought of her as a tall abbess in white robes; he was astonished whenever he found himself holding her in his arms. Her role was to be an apparition for everyone; perhaps, as a woman, she could never wholly commit herself to any man.

So, in Jules's mind, *their* love became, once again, something relative and contingent. His own was absolute.

## 7

## *Magda*

After a few weeks in Paris, Jules rebelled; he tried to break himself of Lucie and began noticing the Parisian girls again. With Jim's help he put an advertisement in the matrimonial column in one of the big dailies. One of those who came to see him as a result was an alert, respectable little woman called Juliette. Jules was filled with wonder by her white stockings, her varnished shoes, her direct, lively glance, and the clockwork precision – and the limitations – of her mind. He and Jim took her out to the theatre.

For as much as twenty-four hours Jules harboured thoughts of marriage. 'This is the only method of approach for me,' he said, 'and besides, I only need to pull it off once.' But the ghost of Lucie came up before him; so he did nothing; and Juliette came no more.

Jules got a long letter from a cousin who was older than himself. A friend, a widow of twenty-five with a little boy, was about to visit Paris. Would Jules like to keep her entertained and show her the Latin Quarter?

Meanwhile she wrote to Jules suggesting he should call on her.

Jules invited Jim to lunch and showed him both letters. They went for a walk in the Tuileries Gardens, in front of the woman's hotel, waiting for the time appointed. 'I really do feel this is different,' said Jules, 'I feel she may be meant for me.' A church clock struck and he set off, his little steps going quicker than normal.

Next morning he told Jim, 'She's quiet and pleasant, she's got a way with her and she's experienced. She's a talented musician. She's not involved with anyone. I'm a bit smitten already. I think she may like me. Will you come to a concert with us this evening?'

'What do you need me for?' said Jim. 'You'll be much happier by yourselves.'

'No, you must come, really,' said Jules, 'I've told her about you already. She wants to meet you. I do need you.'

So Jim went.

Jules introduced him. 'This is Jim. You must pronounce it English-fashion, *Djim* not *Zheem*, it doesn't suit him.'

Magda was just as Jules had described her; she was devoted to her singing, learned without being pedantic. They had supper together. She liked Jules and treated Jim as a friend. She had a way of enveloping you in her own atmosphere.

'At last!' Jim said to himself.

After a month had passed she let Jules take her. 'At last!' Jim said to himself again. He was spending a good deal of time with them and was delighted to see Jules happy. Magda for her part was taking hold of life and beauty again. When she was alone with Jules, or with them both, she no longer dressed or behaved like a widow.

But there were disturbing signs. Jules wrote a poem on *The Matron of Ephesus* and began slipping back a bit into his old ways, his self-devouring cogitations which somehow always resulted in damaging his life, without any action on anyone else's part. Late one evening in the Rue de la Gaîté, in an empty café, he declared, 'What matters is that the woman should be faithful, male fidelity's unimportant.' Jim wondered if he was thinking of Lucie.

Magda had turned pale.

'You're a couple of fools,' she said.

'Maybe,' said Jim. 'But I didn't say anything, and I don't necessarily approve of everything Jules says at 2 a.m.'

'Then disagree with him!' said Magda.

'I disagree,' said Jim.

Jules looked surprised.

'There you see!' said Magda, and taking him by the arm she led him off like a naughty child.

Jim did his best never to see them together. Despite being much preoccupied with his own life at this time, he called on Jules every day.

One morning Jules said to him, 'Magda thinks you're cross with her since she lost her temper at that café. Tonight we're going to try taking ether, to see what it's like. She's invited you to dinner.' He was afraid Jim would refuse.

'Thanks,' said Jim, 'I'll come. But I shan't take much ether, I don't care for that sort of thing.'


Dinner was served on the floor, in little Persian bowls, in front of a big wood fire.

Magda herself had prepared hors-d'oeuvres in the style of her own country. Jules was gay, and read poems aloud in three languages; Magda improvised on her piano. A cold rain was clattering down outside, and it was good to be there by the fire.

Ether-time came.

Armed with wads of cotton-wool, and bottles, they began inhaling deeply. Jim felt it was an offence against his body. 'Exhilarating,' said one of them. 'Exhilarating,' said the other two.

Coolness flooded into their brains and their ears buzzed; the sense of well-being was tremendous. They felt as if they were expanding, like wineskins filling out. At the beginning of each in-breath the smell was unpleasant at first, but soon they began to crave it.

Magda's reactions were big and uninhibited. Jim only half let himself go, while Jules let himself go altogether, with a great expenditure of both cotton-wool and liquid.

The ample supply of cushions became too small for their indolent limbs. Jules suggested that they lie down on Magda's great bed. Which they did. Magda and Jim lay at the sides and left the middle place free for Jules, but he firmly pushed Magda into it and would take no refusal.

Wad after wad of cotton-wool was used, in darkness now. There were long silences. The firelight flickered.

And then suddenly it was as if a mosquito had stung them. Jules brought out a mordant paradox on the duplicity of women, referring to an incident which had been making a stir in the papers.

'Please, Jules,' begged Jim, 'no psychology tonight.'

'Is this supposed to apply to me?' asked Magda.

'Of course,' said Jules, laughing. 'It applies to every woman.'

And he talked away, mocking both himself and Magda and mixing platitudes with wit. They tried to stop him. Jim made an effort to stand up but Magda put out a hand to restrain him. She covered her ears, but Jules stopped talking for a second and took one of her hands away. She let him have his way because she thought he was going to say something pleasant, but he leant over and whispered in her ear, which he would never have done in front of Jim if he hadn't been drunk with ether.

Magda groaned.

'Put on the light, Jim,' she said.

Jim pressed the hanging switch. Magda's face was tense; she was even angrier than she had been in the café.

'Get out, Jules!' she ordered.

Jules was wearing his expression of a baby who has just tortured an insect. The curt command from Magda, a former officer's wife, took effect on him as it would have done on a soldier. He got off the bed, removed the kimono she had lent him, put on his jacket and shoes and went out into the adjoining room. They heard him open the door on the landing and close it behind him.

Jim sat up and was about to follow him, but Magda pulled him down against herself. Desire welled up in her and she twined herself as close to him as she could.

'Magda, you're trying to take revenge on Jules,' said Jim, 'and you'll be sorry.'

'Never! And I'd rather it was you than anyone else.'

'It's true,' thought Jim to himself, 'it'll matter less with me.'

'Not like that!' she said. And began undressing him.

They spent a night of candid and almost impersonal desire, a night impregnated with ether and entirely caused by Jules; a pagan flare-up which was beautiful in its own way, without sequel or after-taste.

In the morning, waking with her head on Jim's shoulder, she said:

'Don't you think Jules wanted us to?'

'He was drunk on ether,' said Jim.

'Yes, but he was more like himself than ever. Let him learn to weigh the consequences of the things he says! Tell him what we've done, will you, please?'

Jim went to see Jules, who couldn't understand why he had been thrown out. Jim told him faithfully, adding at the end, 'We didn't kiss once' – which was true.

Jules went off to see Magda at once; he apologized, she didn't, they were reconciled and had a second honeymoon. They saw Jim as much as before, and no one was embarrassed.

★

Jules and Magda went to stay in the South of France. They sent Jim touching photos in which it looked as if they were out of this world and completely united. Jim had a burst of hope for Jules.

Soon after they got back, Jules said to Jim:

'I love Magda. But it's a habit; it's not a great love, not the real thing. To me, she's like a young mother and an attentive daughter, both at once.'

'But that's fine!'

'It's not the love I've always dreamed of having.'

'Does that kind of love exist?' said Jim.

'Of course! My love for Lucie.'

Jim checked himself from saying, 'Because you don't possess her.'

'Besides,' Jules went on, 'knowing myself as I do, I shall never be able to forgive any woman for loving me. To love me is a sign of perversion or compromise – and Lucie doesn't suffer from either. There's not a particle of me that she accepts.'

'With her, any man could think that.'

'Yes, *could* . . .' said Jules. 'But I *do*.'

'Oh well,' said Jim, 'it's heroic and one can't help respecting it. It's a bit like martyrdom. And it's the key to your life. If Lucie loved you . . .'

'She wouldn't be Lucie,' said Jules.


For eight months the liaison held together, eight months of which some parts were good and sustaining, like bread.

A letter arrived from Lucie, talking of her coming to Paris next summer.

Jules made up his mind to be quite open with Magda about Lucie. So far he had merely intimated that she existed, and Magda had been able to think that it was a thing of the past.

So he told her, reverently – as reverently as he had once lit the stove under his bed.

Two days later Magda went back to her own country.

After a few months she remarried: 'He's a real man, steady and generous,' she wrote; she was happy and she bore Jules no grudge – rather the contrary, in fact.

# 8

## Odile

In the painters' café he frequented, Jules, with Jim, had met an eighteen-year-old girl from one of the Nordic countries. She was called Odile and she liked coming to drink tea with them in Jules's flat; he lived near the café. She said she had married and divorced; she spoke pidgin; she was direct, brutally frank, full of humour, and had a skin like milk.

'Me no understand life men women here. Be opposite to my country. Them here make love when want. This important. Me want learn here.'

Jules, preoccupied at that time by Magda, felt no attraction towards Odile. She amused him and he treated her like a kitten when she came to see him. He played dominoes with her and gave her lessons in zany French. Good marks were rewarded with pipes made of red sugar, which she crunched up noisily and which in those days cost a *sou*.

At the café she had a noisy argument with Jules: 'What! Me say "me fall on MA *derrière*, my bottom", and you want me say "me fall on MON *derrière*". Shocking. Not polite. You Mister: MON *derrière*. Me lady: MA *derrière*. Me say you silly.' And all the regulars were on her side.

One day at Jules's flat she said to him: 'Many them at café want teach me. Me no want. Me rather learn with Jim. What you advise me?'

'Jim good teacher,' said Jules.

'What Jim think about me?'

'Jim think you lovely eyes, lovely mouth, lovely hair, lovely white skin, lovely everything,' said Jules, who had been compelled to adopt her language.

'You think he want teach me?'

'He want.'

'You sure, sure?'

'Me sure, sure.'

'You no want?'

'Me no want.'

'Why you no want?'

'Me want teach other girl.'

'Me know she?'

'You no know she.'

She was about to ask, 'Why me no know she?' but having noticed what the time was she changed the subject:

'Jim come today for tea?'

'Jim come.'

'You lend me and Jim your bedroom today if need?'

'Me lend.'

'For us use altogether?'

'Altogether.'

'You go out when me make sign you?'

'Me go out.'

'You no cross at all?'

'No cross at all.'

They took their dominoes. Jim arrived and they drank tea. Odile set about her seduction scene like a clown, putting on an act for Jules and for herself too. Jim lent himself to it without knowing what it was all about. Odile had liked him at first sight. Jules became a polite official for the occasion, and Odile plied him with questions as if he had been a stage confidant.

She quickly had him in fits of laughter, holding his sides and gasping, 'Stop, stop!' Jim was giving her her cues, in pidgin, but underneath it all he was in earnest. It was on this that Odile, while hiding the fact that she was in earnest too, was building her whole act. When her ridiculous patter and her outrageous questions to Jim had mounted to a climax, she pointed at the door with outstretched forefinger. Suddenly feeling a little sad, Jim took her in his arms.

'We hide under bedclothes,' said Odile. And with a masterful lift of the eyebrows at Jules, she let herself fall whole-heartedly into Jim's embrace.

When Jules came home about midnight he found the remains of a modest dinner neatly arranged on his table, while from his bed came, like an arrow, Odile's cool freshness, mingled with the smell of the fashionable English soap which she always carried in her bag.

The next day Jules and Jim, both working in Jules's flat, heard a high-spirited 'Yoop! Yoop!' through the open window. It was Odile passing by, accompanied by a tall young man who was a compatriot of hers. She had monks' sandals on her bare feet, a long black Spanish cloak, and a big dark blue straw hat of the kind worn by the Salvation Army. They could see right into the back of her healthy throat, and the join of her long white neck and her torso. 'See you in a minute!' she shouted to them.

She came whenever she wanted, which was often, and was always welcome. Jim wondered why she had picked him out instead of one of the handsome young men from her own country. 'But she's said why,' answered Jules. 'She's learning about Latin culture; free morals, without crudity or false modesty. She's got an unerring instinct and knows what she needs. Most women from her country spend their time in Paris in big hotels, with their men, and only get to know French life from the outside.'

'But am I so Latin?' said Jim. 'One of my great-grandfathers was Nordic, I look like his portrait, and I'm even taller than Odile's friends.'

'It's that Nordic one-eighth which makes you just right for her, and also the fact that you lived long enough in her country to take on a veneer of its style.'

'What a mixture she is!'

'I've had more chance of talking to her than you have. On her father's side she's an aristocrat, her mother was of the people. Thanks to that, she's ignorant of anything in between, and to everyone who looks at her she teaches—'

'What does she teach?'

'Shakespeare,' said Jules.

One day Odile took Jim to her place. He didn't know she had one. It was a three-room apartment looking on to a cul-de-sac, in an old house in a humble quarter. The first two rooms were empty, with very clean scrubbed floors and faded flowered wallpaper.

The third room, whose walls were painted with white priming, contained nothing but a large bed consisting of a mattress on the floor, with embroidered blankets; just right for two. The pillows were one on top of the other, not side by side.

Sitting up on the black marble mantelpiece was a row of dolls. On the floor, by the mattress, within easy reach, was a line of creatures, most of them white; some furry, others feathered, some old and worn out, others brand new and of the most elegant quality which Paris and London could produce.

Odile sat on her bed and inspected them. She always behaved as if she was alone, and never did anything but what she wanted. That was why Jules and Jim respected her; and she felt their respect and was at ease with them.

★

She picked up her animals one by one and talked to them, apparently resuming relations with them after an absence of several days. Jim, sitting on the floor with his back to the wall, felt as if he was in a nursery with a little girl. Odile discovered a stain on her white sheep which said *baa* when you squeezed it; she wetted it with petrol and rubbed it with the sleeve of a pair of white silk pyjamas. Then she burnt a letter, the sheep caught fire, and she rolled it up in her coverlet; Jim thought the fire would spread, but it didn't.

Bit by bit he learnt that an elderly neighbour did the housework, that Odile had been living there for several months, possibly with her husband, that she had sold off all her belongings to neighbours and junk-shops except her bedding, dolls and animals, that she liked it much better that way, and that she was going to sell off the rest too and get out with nothing but her suitcases.

Jim was looking for a little place for her and himself, something other than a hotel room. He would gladly have bought all her possessions and taken over the remainder of the lease; these bare rooms were the perfect setting for Odile. But to her they were peopled by ghosts to whom she had now come to say good-bye. It would be quite impossible for him to lie in that bed alongside Odile and her animals.

With Jim's help Odile turned out everything in the cupboards and the kitchen. She held out a bottle which was full of some liquid or other: 'Me take that away.'

'What is it?' said Jim.

She looked serious.

'That be vitriol. That be for eyes of man tell me lies. He come back one day. Me keep that for he. Me learn about that at café. Them girls models say judges always kind and not give big punishment.'

Jim explained that the bottle would get broken among all her other packages, the vitriol would run down and burn her feet; besides, you could buy the stuff everywhere. She said:

'Yes, but not same bottle me swore throw.'

She allowed herself to be talked round and reluctantly poured the liquid down the plug-hole of the sink, where it frothed and bubbled.

As an inactive spectator, keeping a straight face and wishing that Jules had been there, Jim watched the bed-linen and mattress being sold to the neighbours. Odile showed herself to be a surprisingly good businesswoman, at once tactful and quick-witted.

One of the good-looking young men from Odile's crowd came and invited Jim to supper with them. Jim, who knew him very slightly but rather liked him, was going to accept but Odile said, 'No. Me no want mix.'

She went by herself.

Odile explained to Jules, 'Them treat me good, like lady. Jim do that too. But all same he and them be different, me no want one see the other. And maybe they want alter Jim.'

Odile was still 'learning' from Jim, and he found her ways endearing. She turned up when she felt like it, laughing by herself at the Creation and speaking her thoughts out loud. They would have liked to write down what she said, but her presence swamped everything and stopped them.

# 9

## Among the Dunes

Odile and Jim thought it would be fun to spend a fortnight by the sea. Odile wanted to pick Jules up and take him with them, Jim liked the idea and Jules wanted nothing better.

They took the train lightheartedly, travelling second class because there was no third, to Amsterdam, which amused them, particularly the solemn cafés. Never had Odile and Jules handled such big dominoes.

The house agents had nothing left to let by the sea. Jim had to bicycle for two days along the coast before he found the dream house: isolated, tucked among the sand dunes, swept by the wind, white inside and out, and without furniture.

When, after midnight, Jim came back to their little hotel and climbed the ladder-like stair to their ship's cabin of a room, he found Odile sleeping pillowed on his neatly folded pyjamas. She looked an angel.

The light woke her. 'Me good girl, me go to bed by myself,' she said.

Jules came in shaking a finger at her: 'Because me no want you in my bed.'

'You being stupid,' said Odile. 'You not understand me want be in your bed because me not have animals and me not like sleep all alone . . . but me be good girl for Jim!'

'But maybe me not good boy!' put in Jules.

She stared at him, outraged.

They moved into the little house, hired two mattresses, three chairs, a table and some saucepans. Odile slept downstairs in the one big room, and Jules up in the attic. A small kitchen also did as a bathroom.

Odile turned out to be a housewife, in her own way. She washed the floor thoroughly twice a week, though afterwards she strewed it with peach-stones and banana skins and the remains of figs, which skidded underfoot at night. She said, 'That not dirty. And me have the right because me wash.'

Jules and Jim, pipes in mouths, went to market and brought back milk and baskets of vegetables. It was their moment together. The fishermen came to the door with fish; Odile received them in a pair of pyjamas with a hole in the seat and told them fantastic stories of which they didn't understand a word. The trio were known locally as the three lunatics, but apart from that were accepted.

It was, at first, a blissful life. Odile was happy all the time. Jim bathed in her blondeness at night and the sea by day. Jules played for hours with Odile, then went off to his attic to work on a novel, his chair on the trap-door which led up there, to prevent Odile from bursting in.

Jules took Odile and Jim their morning coffee and toast in bed. He thought this charming but violent love-affair would be brief. More and more Odile's nights belonged to Jim and her days to Jules.

At mealtimes Jim was sometimes tired and Odile was horrid to him. As Jules refused to take her side, she was angry with both of them and called them, 'Stuffy little artists. Worthless writers. Grocers.' They laughed; Jules said, 'No doubt you're right. We do our best.'

Odile got a bundle of letters from Paris and her own country. She didn't talk about them but after these letters she became severe to Jim and Jules.

One day she wanted to buy six large live lobsters from the fishermen, to play with; a beautiful but expensive idea. Jim explained their small budget wouldn't stand it. She accused him angrily of being mean. She wasn't afraid of living simply but she was used to getting windfalls to spend on her fantasies. She backed horses, by post, in Paris and London.

The laundress came, having lost some linen. Odile violently took her side.

Bathing that morning, she splashed about as usual, walking parallel to the waves. But she moved further and further off along the sandy shore, became a dot on the horizon, and disappeared. Jules and Jim lunched and dined alone, without worrying to start with, because even at the height of her follies Odile always kept her head.

That evening there was a gentle knock on the door. It was Odile in her swimsuit, escorted by two policemen. She had gone right along to a seaside resort a mile away, walked through the streets just as she was, which was against the regulations, and drawn crowds. The police were most unwilling to put her in prison this time, but in future Jim and Jules would be held responsible for her behaviour; they could be fined and expelled from the country.

Odile, quite at ease, was acutely interested by the whole account as Jules translated it sentence by sentence. The younger of the policemen said, 'She's mad – or else very naughty.'

In her turn, laughing and voluble, Odile told the story of her escapade. She ended, 'Middle-class women of town not pretty, jealous because husbands look at me. They say, put gipsy in prison.'

No one referred to the incident after this. But now and then Odile suddenly declared war on both her companions.

One day, thirsting for revenge, she really tried to seduce Jules, and failed. Jim had nothing against it. He had had his share. He would have taken his turn in the attic.

Odile determined to poison them. When they had started on the fatal omelette she said, 'You no find it got funny taste? You no suspicion your cook? You been walking on her face. You no understand she furious? She nice girl, she tell you: Stop eat that!'

But they had colic all the same.

The fortnight went bumping along to its end. On their way back they passed through a city, where Odile bought four pairs of wooden shoes. Jules and Jim rashly left her alone, eating ices in front of a shop window; on returning they found her indignant, draped in her Spanish cloak, the string of wooden shoes over her shoulder, surrounded by a crowd as if she had been a street-singer, and ticking them off politely: 'What you want with me? Why you look at me like animal in zoo? You never seen anything? You not very civilized. You go on like this, me call police. What funny about me? Nose? Mouth? Cloak? Wood shoes?' (She pointed to each in turn.) 'When Jim and Jules come back them smack your heads for sure. Them come now!'

No one could understand her. Jules and Jim came up, the crowd dispersed; they went off to the station, and the children following them dropped away.

In Paris Odile went back with relief to her compatriots, disappearing for a fortnight; after which she turned up, kissed Jim and Jules and took to visiting them again, but less often than before. Sometimes she invited Jim to come home with her by giving him her bottle of milk to carry, in the café at about midnight.

She had found the right dose now.

Jules told Odile of Lucie's imminent arrival and asked her not to come and see him for a few days.

## 10

# *Lucie in Paris*

Lucie was lying on Jules's divan, propped on cushions. They were talking quietly, recreating their atmosphere.

The bell rang but Jules didn't answer it. It rang again, loudly, and the man from the other flat on the same floor went to see who it was. Jules's door flew open and there, even more pale and blonde than Lucie, was Odile in her cloak. She came in, shutting the door behind her.

'Ah! You be Lucie! Jules tell me no come when you here. So me come a-purpose! Me very curious about you. Me glad know you, even if you no glad know me . . . You be Jules's woman-friend or his fiancy?'

'That's enough, Odile,' said Jules, 'leave us now.'

'Me no leave at all,' said Odile.

Jules leaped up, putting one arm round her bosom and the other under her calves, and carried her out, despite her attempts to hang on with feet and hands on the way through the door.

She was shouting, 'Oh, how he love she! He real man for once. He strong, he nearly beat me.'

Jules put her down on the landing and came back, locking the door.

'Tell me about Odile,' said Lucie.

Jules did, not mentioning Odile's affair with Jim to begin with; but Lucie guessed: 'She's so young and alive and bold, I'm sure Jim couldn't resist, any more than he could with Gertrude.'

Jim wanted Lucie to know about his adventure with Odile; so Jules told the story, *à la* Jules.

Lucie listened gravely, smiling sometimes with Jules. Then she said:

'I'd like to have tea with you and Jim and Odile next week. Can that be arranged?'

'Of course,' said Jules.

After being thrown out by Jules, Odile ran off to the café and waited for Jim.

'Marvellous!' she said, 'me seen Lucie at Jules's flat. He beat me, she see. She big chief woman! She no move on sofa, no speak, not lift eyebrow. Me take good look at she while me being beaten. She stronger than me, she win this time. But me revenge!'

And off she ran again.

Jim would have liked to be there when all this happened; however, Jules and Lucie would tell him about it. It had been settled that Lucie should first see Jules alone, that afternoon, and Jim would go and see her in the evening, after dinner.

On his way, he felt a sudden urgent need to be with her again. He entered the quiet little *pension* and began climbing two flights of wooden stairs towards her room; he knew where it was and had seen that its two windows were lit up.

He heard light footsteps catching him up and felt one of his legs gripped by two arms. It was Odile; she had shadowed Lucie from Jules's flat to the *pension* and had then come to talk to Jim at the café; after which she had hidden, having doubts, and had followed Jim to the *pension* and come in behind him.

Full of determination, delighted with her success, sitting on a step and looking up at him with her blue eyes, she launched into one of the cross-examinations which he loved so much:

'You go see Lucie?'

'Yes.'

'No. You no go. You staying with me. Me be your woman for tonight. You in love to Lucie?'

'Me friend to Lucie.'

He gave a wrench to free his leg, but merely succeeded in lugging Odile on to the next step. He tried to unfasten her hands.

'Jim, you listen me! If she only your friend, why she no see you in drawing-room like proper lady? Why bedroom? Me allow in drawing-room, with me. If you want go up bedroom and me no there, me make scandal straight away, me yell Lucie your mistress, me say me your poor fiancy. Me make big scene. No good reputation Lucie.'

Jim knew that Odile would do all of this. She was regarded as a lunatic by the neighbourhood and had nothing to lose; but Lucie had a great deal. He thought fast. Odile mustn't get to know Lucie's secrets, she'd make much too much use of them. Amused by Odile's bold move, he gave in:

'All right. But I must leave a note for Lucie, she's been waiting for me.'

'All right,' she echoed.

They went down to the drawing-room, where he wrote that it was 'unfortunately impossible for him to pay his respects' to Lucie that evening.

'Very very good,' said Odile, reading over his shoulder. 'You come.'

She gave the letter to the *concierge* and let Jim take her arm all the way to her room.

Jim was thinking that he and Lucie had plenty of time and that matters between him and Odile would soon die a natural death. He gave himself up to Odile.

In the morning he went to see Jules, and they exchanged news of yesterday's doings. Jules was sad on Lucie's behalf.

'You're so easily swayed Jim,' he said, almost severely.

'Very easily,' said Jim.

'Odile would never have dared do that to me.'

Jules was proud of having put her out by force, in front of Lucie, and Jim was astonished at this incredible departure from Jules's ordinary ways.

Jules went on:

'I demand too much of women, that's why I get nothing from them.'

'What about Magda?'

'She wanted to change me and adapt me to suit herself. You get women all right, but they possess you.'

'Yes,' said Jim, 'and it's only fair that they should. But who possesses a woman more, the man who takes her or the one who just contemplates her?'

'One's got to do both,' said Jules.

In the afternoon Jim came back to Jules's flat to meet Lucie; Jules went out soon after so as to leave them alone. Lucie had been surprised to get Jim's note, which she was told he had 'brought with a lady' on the previous evening. The scene on the stairs had gone unobserved at the *pension*.

Jim kissed Lucie's hands but didn't dare to get as far as her face. He had just been to the gymnasium he frequented, where, as if to punish himself, he had had a specially hard bout in the ring. Despite having a shower afterwards he still felt redolent of Odile, and in Lucie's presence this gave him a pang. Easily swayed, said Jules . . . He told Lucie about Odile, slurring nothing over, and implying that he put her on a lower level than Lucie.

'Don't,' said Lucie, 'you mustn't. She's so pretty and so primitive.'

Jim could feel the affection coming across from Lucie to himself; it was of a kind which kept him chaste when he was with

her. He could also feel Lucie's patience, which had an a
frightening quality.

Jules came in and soon had them lively and gay.

Jim was tired after his bout and asked if he might lie on the
carpet, as if it had been grass; he was told he could. One of his
shoulders was right on the floor, the other one nearly.

'Look at this chap who's always putting women on their backs!'
said Jules, who had moved across and was standing over him.
'Here's a chance of making him touch the ground with both
shoulders.'

'Why not try?' said Lucie.

'May I?' said Jules shyly.

'Yes,' said Jim affectionately.

Jules took aim and pounced with his whole weight on the
raised shoulder, but Jim twisted, rolled Jules over and forced his
shoulders instantly to the floor.

'I should have known it.' Jules was proud of Jim. 'How clever
he is!'

'No,' said Jim, 'I've only just taken up wrestling.'

'What about boxing?' asked Lucie.

'Boxing? Self-defence,' said Jim. 'I like boxing in the same way
as I like chess.'

He was astonished to find that Lucie wanted to see him box.
Had boxing ever entered her horizon?


That night Jim slept at home, at his mother's flat, which he shared
fifty-fifty with her, and where he never received any friends from
his usual stamping-grounds. Jules and he didn't like the atmosphere of the flat for hob-nobbing together. But it was a
wonderful sanctuary for Jim to work in. Even Odile had never
broken into it.

He thought of introducing Lucie to his mother.

*

Lucie invited Jules, Jim and Odile to come and take tea with her, as she had planned. Odile, who was gratified, rehearsed in front of Jim so as to be sure she knew how to behave according to the highest Parisian standards.

The occasion took place in a cosmopolitan *pâtisserie*. Odile talked about her excellent but interrupted education and behaved herself alternately as an exotic princess and a street-child. Lucie left her the initiative and Odile made full use of it. Her face, which was as long as Lucie's, was aristocratic, and her voice showed breeding, but her facial expressions were crude; she was like Hogarth's *Shrimp Girl*, whereas Lucie might have been one of Goethe's grand-daughters.

Jules and Jim were highly entertained, but they were also afraid lest Odile produce some outburst which would cause pain to others in general and Lucie in particular; so they spent an hour on tenterhooks.

Odile almost stopped being jealous of Lucie on Jim's account, because Lucie's manner was so impeccable; besides, she could see how greatly Jules loved Lucie.

Odile declared later that Lucie was very beautiful, but was afraid of 'doing different'.

Jim looked at Lucie's calm hands. Odile had little hands like claws or pincers. Everything she did was larger than life-size, to attract attention, and while her clowning looked something like genius when you met it for the first time it now seemed to him stale and limited, like the portraits she drew with ten strokes of a pencil.

Jules's conversation was brilliant and concise. Remembering the evening with Gertrude, Lucie thought one mustn't let him 'drag his feet', as Gertrude put it – and as Odile encouraged him to do. It seemed to Lucie that Odile wouldn't suit Jim permanently any more than Gertrude had done.

Once they were sure everything was going to pass off

successfully, Jules and Jim enjoyed Odile's shameless questions and the art with which Lucie met them with non-committal answers.

Jules, not without emotion, felt the concealed attention which Jim was paying to Lucie.

## Lucie and Odile

Odile said to Jim:

'Me like you meet my ex-husband.'

'All right,' said Jim.

She took him to a long, narrow, glazed studio. The ex-husband was very young, on the effeminate side, and spoke quickly and precisely; Jim rather liked him. They drank tea, played chess and drew their game; Odile, who was totally ignorant of chess, gave them both advice.

The ex-husband said to Jim:

'Odile has told me about you and I know what place you occupy in her life. Congratulations. Only I ought to let you know that during the last few days, as it happens, Odile and I have revived the past and – resumed marital relations.'

Jim had a glimpse of a stool flying backwards and Odile flying forwards almost horizontally, stretched out like a spring released, with her merciless little hands reaching out to seize her ex-husband by the throat and hurl him over backwards. The oil-lamp rolled on the floor but didn't go out; Jim rescued it and turned it up, to reveal the ex-husband flat on his back and Odile astride on top of him:

'You promised you say nothing!'

'Well, it's done now, anyway,' he said.

He had prised off Odile's hands and got them under control. Both of them got up, and he dusted his clothes calmly.

The two men hesitated, shook hands, and Odile left with Jim.

This confirmed how determined she was to hide her other men from him.

She took Jim to her hotel. On the way they bought things for dinner, and the little white and grey parcels of groceries and fruit made Jim's pocket bulge.

It was cold. 'We'll make a big fire,' she said. She undressed, sat down naked on the floor with her legs apart and a foot pressed against the wall on each side of the fireplace, grabbed lumps of coal from the scuttles, knocked them happily against one another, talking to them meanwhile and covering the carpet with shiny black splinters, and in less than no time had built a high, roaring fire. As she had rubbed her hands on her body now and then, she was striped with black. She asked Jim to put the light out, and in the glow from the fire amused herself by warming herself from every angle, so close to the flames that Jim was afraid she would burn herself. She swept up the coal splinters and ran naked to the bathroom which served the whole of that floor; the door was next to her own.

She was fresh and cool when she came back, the picture of innocence; she got into bed, called Jim, and set about making him forget her ex-husband.

'How important lighting a fire becomes,' Jim was thinking, 'when she does it! She does things one at a time, thoroughly. Jules makes out that she's like her near-namesake Ondine, and has no soul. But how restful!'

Jim and Jules took Lucie and Odile to the *Bal des Quat-z'Arts*. Lucie was dressed as a priestess; Odile was undressed as a native girl, with a raffia scarf. For the first hour Odile was frightened and couldn't believe her eyes; she had never dreamed of such a celebration, and she hung on Jim's arm. Then, as women on men's shoulders began to emerge riding high above the crowd, she climbed on to Jim's; he could feel her thighs pressed against his ears, and he carried her about in the growing tumult. She was getting excited and beginning to talk non-stop.

Jim saw two young men who were talking together and who had noticed Odile. She must have signalled to them, for they came over and introduced themselves to him; one was American, the other a Russian prince from a province which produced a great many princes. They both had fine costumes and fine muscles. They offered to carry Odile if Jim was tired.

'What do you say, Odile?' asked Jim.

'Me glad have three biggest horses at ball,' said Odile, 'and be able change when me like!'

So she got on to the American's shoulders and then the Russian's and was taken wherever she wanted to go; and from time to time she came back to make a trip on Jim's. 'She's made a good choice,' thought Jim, and re-joined Jules and Lucie. The three of them went into one of the cubicles giving on to a studio, where a ring of people were watching a Lesbian exhibition taking place on the floor. Lucie didn't understand at first, she thought it was some kind of eccentric wrestling contest between two naked women; but when she got a better view she gave a groan and asked Jim and Jules to go away.

The bands were already striking up famous marches, and the great parade of tableaux, mounted on chariots, began to move past. The naked figures triggered off a reaction among the crowd; there were sounds of ripping cloth, and the American and the Russian had a hard job to protect Odile's tiny loincloth; her raffia scarf had gone long ago. All the models in Paris were there, and others who weren't models but were rebels against convention, and artists' wives, and women who, like Lucie, had come to watch but weren't really part of it all.

Lucie attracted a good many glances, but only once did Jules and Jim have to ward off an encroaching hand. She was happy to be experiencing all this in their company; she watched with an astonished smile.

Odile's two steeds, having left her behind somewhere, came and asked Jim politely if they and some friends could keep her with them for supper.

'If she wants to,' said Jim. 'But be careful, wine makes her sick.'

'All right,' said the Russian. 'We don't want to spoil her evening or ours.'

'Or yours,' added the American.

Lucie, Jules and Jim had a light supper on their own, in peace. Lucie was worried about Odile.

'She only does what she wants, and she's safe wherever she goes,' said Jules, and Jim agreed.

The beauty contest came on. Women in the nude, mostly models, with their faces made up and their bodies smooth with talc, appeared one after the other for a quarter of a minute on a platform jutting out from the balcony, and the volume of applause expressed the verdict of the crowd. To his surprise Jim noticed, from a distance, Odile in the queue of those waiting their turn. Without letting himself be seen he went up closer. She had a hard, set expression which made her seem like a stranger. She had kept her miniature loincloth; it was now ripped off, in accordance with the rules, and she stepped out on to the platform, under the blinding convergent sheaf of lights. She adopted the traditional pose of the modest Venus, but a hand pulled her own hand away. She made no resistance but stood there for a moment, all her energy bracketed on this new experience. Her delicately moulded beauty didn't show to the best advantage; in this setting, a more emphatic type of figure was needed. She was given no time to strike up her song; an ovation rang out, in which Jim could hear the voice of the Russian.

'How brave she is!' Jules was saying. Lucie was sorry for her. Jim was thinking, 'Graceful body . . . faithless angel . . . she could leave me or I could leave her, and neither of us would bat an eyelid.'

There were drunks, and yells, and a scene breaking out here and there. Dancing began again. A few couples were leaving.

Jim went round the room, half hoping not to find Odile; and he didn't find her. 'Let her learn!' he said to himself. Lucie was sorry they had missed her. Jules had passed a night of happiness at Lucie's side. He and Jim saw her home.

At the café the next night Odile came and sat down beside Jim.

'Why you let me go with other man?'

'Which one, Odile?'

'Russian.'

'Because you wanted to, Odile.'

'Me want to because you no stop me.'

'Me never stop you, Odile.'

'Then you no love me.'

'Me love you in my own way.'

'Your way make me sleep with he. What was you thinking?'

'Me thinking you come back in less than week.'

'He very good, good lover, very very good.'

'Why you no stay with him?'

'Me have enough like that. Me want to see own room again.'

And she gave him her bottle of milk to carry.

Should he refuse? No, because he was curious to know what would happen after. But how would he feel if she held out her bottle to someone else, in front of him – which she had never done? Well, she gave him only part of herself, and he did the same. Would she have preferred a domineering, jealous lover? It wouldn't have been hard for her to find one. He was jealous of this Russian, but he left Odile as free as he himself wanted to be. That was part of the reason why she kept on coming back to him.

In her room she showed him the Russian's elegant visiting card, threw it into her chamber-pot (which she had scrubbed out and converted into a cabinet for addresses and loveletters), and said to Jim, quite seriously:

'We rub out that Russian?'

They rubbed him out.

She went off for a motoring trip with her fellow-countrymen, 'For always, maybe,' she said.

## 12

## *Lucie's Travels*

Lucie and Jim set out on a journey at random, without planning a route. Jules came and put then into their train, with a little basket of choice fruit to keep them company. In a town in Brittany, they discovered an ancient inn close by the cathedral, right opposite the façade. On the top floor a room jutted out, supported over empty space by two brackets of timber and seeming to fly towards the great rose-window. This was Lucie's room. Jim's was directly below hers. He didn't spend much time in it. The big bass bell bathed them in its tingling vibrations.

One hot day they went for an excursion on bicycles to a small deserted church standing on a hillock and surrounded by trees. They walked hand in hand in the cool churchyard, reading touching inscriptions on the tombstones of couples who seemed to have lived peaceful, united lives. They sat down in silence. Jim couldn't bear to leave; he would have liked to stay in the churchyard for ever, lying in a tomb with Lucie at his side . . . However, they had to get back.

The way was long, and at times strenuous. By taking care of her strength and having a rest now and then, Lucie managed it all right. She wasn't as frail as Jim feared. However, for a short time, she had a migraine. If Jim got very tired he had worse ones. He thought to himself, 'If we had children they would be tall and thin and have migraine.'

They went for leisurely walks in the woods, taking a meal with them; Lucie laid it out on the moss. Jim had his gun slung over his shoulder but didn't use it.

Sometimes for fun, they imagined their ideal country house – their future home, no doubt, if they ever had one – down to the last detail of the furniture and garden. In Lucie's fantasy the house had lines and colours, but Jim built with lines alone.

They had a passion for beautiful things made of leather and bought them for each other.

They moved further south, and Jim took Lucie out shooting on the sea, in a sailing dinghy with an old sailor in attendance. It was an entertaining, beautiful kind of shooting. Lucie was as fine and delicate as the most delicate bird. Jim was seized with pity at the sight of the birds' dead bodies as they lay bleeding on the floorboards of the boat. He stopped shooting, and Lucie smiled to him.

There was a slight accident; for a minute Jim thought he had lost an eye. With his other eye he could see that Lucie, had it been possible, would have given him one of hers.

They discovered, behind a pine-forest, a little rural community. Any couple, provided all the others approved of them, could acquire for a small sum a little house of freshly-hewn wood, with an alcove containing two big beds built into the framework (Jim thought of Odysseus's bed), a fireplace which drew well, and a sandy garden capable of growing a few potatoes. Fish was plentiful and would have completed the food supply. A simple life like that was what Jim wanted, but he hadn't the decision to snatch it when the chance offered.

Lucie was afraid of physical love.

Being with her was like being with an abbess, and he wondered if he would be able to go on loving her always. She offered certainty; she was the narrow way. But there was a part of his nature which demanded obstacles to climb, risks to take, and he found fault with himself for it.

One day Lucie and Jim were caught in a storm on the river. Wind, rain and current were against them; Jim was rowing with all his strength but couldn't make headway. Lucie, who was steering, went forward, took the second pair of oars, settled herself without fuss and fitted in her own slight efforts so well with Jim's, without a single clash of oars, that they managed to get back.

From time to time they talked about Jules. In a letter to them both, he invited Lucie to spend a week with him by the sea. 'It would be all right,' said Lucie, 'if I was sure he didn't still want to marry me.' Jim hoped Lucie would accept.

Their last day came. They had had a month, and it was carved in their memories by all the small and perfect things they had enjoyed together.

They parted on the verge of tears, but there was nothing forcing them to part at all.

The day before setting off with Lucie, Jules said to Jim:

'Lucie and I will be bathing together. My back and chest are . . . hairy' (he hesitated before saying the word). 'Some women like that, but I'm sure Lucie doesn't. I don't want to go to one of those "institutes". I started doing the job on my own but I couldn't manage it. Jim, will you help me?' and out of his pocket he pulled a large pot of depilatory cream.

Jim realized that Jules, who had often seen him naked in the shower, had always hidden his own body from him. Jim now saw that Jules was compact and sturdy, like a Roman legionary, with a mat of black curling hair – quite different from the smooth slimness of Odile and Lucie and of Jim himself, but well built all the same.

Why did Jules dislike his own physical type and refuse to marry his pretty cousin? She was willing, she was like him, and they would have been a well-matched couple.

Wasn't it because Lucie resembled him too closely – was too

much his sister, physically speaking, that Jim was so hesitant to make her his wife?

Jim removed the hair from Jules's back. It was rather fun; first you had to melt the sticky cream, spread it out well over the hair and let it dry for a moment; then you pulled it off in one piece, with a sharp jerk. Little by little, Jules's contours emerged more sharply.

How could Lucie react?

Of course it was hopeless, but Jim could have wished that Jules would sweep her off her feet.

Lucie and Jules spent a peaceful week together. He was reserved, and Lucie was grateful to him. After a swim she gave him her feet to dry. Jules was able to sunbathe beside her without embarrassment. He was trying to keep himself satisfied by visits to a blonde girl who lived at a house of assignation in the neighbouring town. And he wrote several new poems for Lucie.

She unburdened herself of her anxieties about Jim. She both admired and feared his freedom.

'As soon as Jim wants to do anything,' said Jules, 'and to the extent that he doesn't think it will hurt anybody else (he could be wrong there, though), he does it, for the pleasure and because he wants to learn something from the experience. He hopes that one day he'll achieve wisdom.'

'Surely that may take a long time?'

'We can't tell,' said Jules. 'Neither can he. After all, he might have a revelation.'

'Really!' said Lucie one day, 'you seem to think that Jim's chaste.'

'But of course he is,' said Jules. 'All really passionate men are. He's chaster than I am, and than most other men. I've known him go without a woman for months, without even looking for one. He's not the sort that runs after someone passing in the street. What he's mad about, what he worships, is character, and he doesn't go for sensuality in itself. Lina, with the façade she puts up, wasn't a character: he turned away from her instinctively. But you're one, Lucie. So are Gertrude and Odile.' (He thought to himself, 'Magda was only half a character, that's why she fell to my share.') 'You're a unity, and so's Jim. I'm faint with love for one thing after another in you – your feet, your hands, your lips. Direct personalities always see the other person as a whole. Some people would say Jim was always making women fall for him, but really it's he who does the falling and they who make him do it. You and Gertrude and Odile, you all chose him before he chose you.'

'Or perhaps it was at the same time?' said Lucie.

After this, Lucie went off to the mountains for a few days with a young man from her own country who was in love with her, and whose photograph she had shown to Jules and Jim. Jules thought there wasn't the same natural intimacy between her and this man as between her and Jim, but that he might become a danger if Jim were to disappear from the scene.

Lucie went home to her father's house.

# 13

## The Archaic Smile

Jules and Jim went to Greece.

For months they had been preparing for this journey at the Bibliothèque Nationale. Jules had ferreted out the essential books for Jim. When Jim was tired of reading he went and joined Jules, whom he found surrounded with large plans of ruined temples; Jim would then reconstruct them with the help of the books. Jules had polished up his ancient Greek and had embarked on learning modern Greek.

They set off with the minimum of luggage. They had had suits made for themselves, of the same light cloth and in the same style. At Marseille they took ship for Naples. Jim lay at the very tip of the bows and watched the stem cutting the blue water. Jules re-read his ponderous tomes and came to explain important points to Jim from time to time. They were sharing a cabin; Jim had the top bunk and Jules the lower, directly underneath. They talked at night as well as by day. They liked it whenever chance put them in a single room, though they always asked for separate ones.

Jim was interested in the origin of the small, neat, circular incision which runs round a Doric column, just under the capital.

At Naples, Jim was fascinated by the 'Venus girdles' in the aquarium, those little creatures whose tissues are diaphanous and almost invisible, and which have a ring of rainbow colours inside them, half-way along their bodies.

They visited the museum of antiquities very thoroughly. They went to see Paestum, with its three temples, and the Greek miracle entered their lives.

Jules got to know a Neapolitan girl, and sent her flowers and sweets.

Next came Sicily – Palermo and its mosaics, and Segeste with its temple, which they visited on foot, disdaining to avail themselves of donkey-transport. They felt they were pilgrims, and a tiring day was well worthwhile for the sake of the beautiful things they saw. Jules recited Homer. At Selinonte they saw the remains of the giant temples which had fallen in earthquakes as corn falls before the sickle, and whose layout they had studied in Paris. Jules so much enjoyed rebuilding them for Jim that when they found one which was still standing up, he exclaimed, 'What a pity!'

Syracuse, the *fons Arethusa* – such names were a delight to Jim.

They embarked on a squalid little cargo ship with four cabins smelling of toothpaste and frying-fat. A gale rose and went on for five days. Jim, who had never been seasick, felt uncomfortable; he lay on his bunk and read, eating nothing. Jules ate every meal and was alternately euphoric and depressed; the cook said to him things like, 'Well, sir, you managed to keep that steak down for an hour; you're coming on.'

Crete shone in the sunshine, and on a calm sea they turned northward. They watched intently. Jules was the first to see, on the horizon, a tiny pale flicker which was the Acropolis.

Their month in Athens was alive with pagan religious fervour; they felt like Greeks. Temples and museums poured a sense of beauty into them.

The Wingless Victory reminded them of Lucie; a female combatant on a pediment, of Gertrude; and a dancing girl on a vase, of Odile.

They explored Cape Sunion on foot, under a fierce sun; Jim

refused to eat or drink or smoke, and displayed as much endurance that day as Jules. Tiryns also they visited on foot, and Mycenae, where the royal palace and its heaps of marble blocks were an overwhelming experience.

Jules, who stroked the statues he saw, wanted living contacts as well. They inquired of an old guide whom Jules had rebuffed on the first day, and whom it now took him a long time to find. They spent an evening in the only bar in Athens where there was any real night life – and where they found women of every nationality except Greek! But there was a girl from one of the Teutonic countries who had the Greek looks and physique and was like a younger edition of Gertrude. Jules made a date with her for the next day, at noon. He was like a cat on hot bricks till the time came, and spent great care on his appearance; when he presented himself, a maid said, 'Madame came home at nine o'clock this morning and told me not to wake her.' Jules made off, deeply disconsolate.

'It's not surprising,' Jim told him, 'considering the life she leads and the amount of champagne she drinks. She doesn't mean anything by it; she was nice to you the day before yesterday, and she will be again tonight.'

'No,' said Jules, 'it's finished. I wanted her now.'

Jules was expecting the arrival of a compatriot, a friend from university days who was now a painter with a promising future. 'He's married – to Hellas,' said Jules.

Albert arrived. He knew even more Greek than Jules. He was tall and dark-skinned, not good-looking, but a character. He showed them his collection of sketches and photos, one of which was of a goddess being abducted by a hero. She had an archaic smile which made a great impression on them. The statue, which had been excavated recently, was on one of the islands, and they decided to go and see it together.

They went out as a trio, frequenting the same *pâtisserie* on a terrace in the park as the bourgeoisie of Athens. They kept their eyes open for faces of the ancient Greek mould, but they never saw one.

Together they went for a tour in the Peloponnese. Albert was a strict, demanding teacher, and under his guidance they saw things thoroughly. Jim respected him but was jealous of his influence over Jules; when he realized he was jealous he pulled himself together. He drank in Albert's superior knowledge but disliked his smiling dogmatism.

At Delphi, as the mules they had ordered didn't arrive, they set off through the mountains on little thin donkeys, with a child as guide, in low cloud and driving rain. They lost their way, and the hard saddles made them sore; they stopped at a wretched, isolated inn, where they found a couple of bedbugs even under the pot of stew on the table. To protect himself against these creatures Albert got into a special light sleeping-bag which muffled him from neck to feet, like a clown. They played poker to kill time, managed to get some sleep somehow, and set off again.

There was a danger of typhoid from the drinking-water, and the tea at the inns was badly made, so they drank resinated wine. Jim got a touch of dysentery and was irritable and jumpy. One day, at lunch, Albert favoured them yet again with his views on the universe, views implying his conviction that his own race was superior to all others.

Jim, who had been restraining himself for some time, broke out angrily at this and tried to get him to take back what he said. They might have fought, but Jules's calm presence prevented them. Albert was astonished and Jim recovered his politeness.

A toy steamer took them to the island; they hurried to their statue and spent an hour with it. It was beyond even what they had hoped. They lingered round the goddess in silence, gazing at her from different angles; her smile was a floating presence, powerful, youthful, thirsty for kisses and perhaps for blood.

They didn't mention her to each other till the next day. Had they ever met such a smile? Never. What would they do if they did meet it one day? Follow it.

Albert proceeded on his travels; Jules and Jim went back to Paris, full of the revelation they had just received, and feeling sure that the divine was within human reach.

## I4

## *The Crows*

Paris gently took charge of them again. Odile had gone back to her own country for good. Jules took a small flat and they furnished it together. Jim designed the big double bed which Jules had set his heart on having; it was low, with a semi-circular disc at the head and the foot, and he bought the best bedding to be had in Paris.

Whom was Jules going to put into it? Well, they'd see.

They had had enough of the cafés; they worked, sometimes together, sometimes alone. Jules's last novel had been fairly successful. In it he had described, in a fairytale atmosphere, some of the women he had known, before Jim's time and even Lucie's.

Jim had a private emotional life of his own which was entirely French and which didn't intersect the field of their friendship; Jules didn't want to be concerned in it in any way.

Jules went to stay for a month at a house in Burgundy which belonged to Jim's mother. They were alone together. It was autumn. On foot, with red and brown leaves falling round them, they made a pilgrimage to Vézelay. Jules acted as beater, driving hares to Jim's gun, and Jim sometimes killed one.

One afternoon they went for a long walk over the flat, deserted, snowy country. A flock of crows was soaring and wheeling overhead. Jim told Jules to wrap himself completely in his long brown cape, lower the hood and run forward with a limp, falling down after every twenty steps or so and lying motionless for a moment, like a dying animal. Jules played the part well. Jim, who had hidden a little way off, saw the crows form up in a great whirling disc and follow Jules; the middle of the disc began to come down like an inverted waterspout, whose apex came closer and closer to Jules. Jules couldn't see this happening.

Suddenly it was very close: the flock was a vortex near to the ground, about to dive on Jules. Jim was afraid for him; in his imagination he saw Jules lifting his hood as the crows enveloped him, and getting pecked in the eyes.

He jumped out of his hiding-place and fired. The crows hardly faltered. He ran, firing again. The crows drew away reluctantly.

Jules was pleased at the success of his trick; but Jim was stirred, as if by some symbol which was beyond his comprehension.

They visited Romanic churches. The image of Lucie which they conjured up in these churches was more like the real Lucie than the one they had evoked on the Acropolis.

# PART 2

*Kate*

# I

## Kate and Jules

Paris.

Jules announced that a new cargo of girls was expected from his country – from Berlin, this time. Jim would have preferred not to see them and to go on working in peace, but Jules explained that he was part of the programme and that he could help them a great deal without giving up much of his time.

There were three of them, and they were decidedly on the lookout for fun. 'They don't need us at all,' thought Jim, 'and they're very experienced for their age.' They began painting with passionate absorption, and seemed nevertheless to have become familiar with Paris in their first week.

The first, Sarah, was tall and dark; a stern, Asiatic beauty. The second, dimpled and lively, was a Viennese beauty. The third was very fair, with a brown sunburned skin; a Germanic beauty. They caused a sensation whenever they entered a dance-hall together.

Kate, the third, had the smile of the statue on the island.

She was the one Jim had specially noticed, and Jules saw her alone every day on his own. He didn't invite Jim to meet her. This went on for a month.

On his visits to Jim he remained secretive, which Jim interpreted as a good sign. He said to Jim:

'Come and spend the evening of the 14th of July with Kate

and me, we'd both like it, but –' (he looked Jim in the face and spoke quietly and slowly) '– not that one? Eh, Jim?'

'All right, Jules,' said Jim, 'not that one.'

At Jules's place Jim found Kate disguised as a young man, in one of Jules's suits. She had broad shoulders and slim hips; a cloth cap hiding her hair (which she wore piled on top of her head); big yellow leather gloves; and a bold, cheeky air. Anyone not in the know might have thought she was a boy, for a moment.

'What do you say about our friend Tom,' said Jules, 'is he fit for us to go out with tonight?'

Jim had a good look at Tom, made them add a faint moustache and let down his trousers a bit, and said:

'That's got it.'

'Now for a try-out in the street!' demanded Tom.

They went down the Boul' Mich' together and stopped at the dances in progress at every crossroads. Jules and Tom danced together. Now and then, remarks were flung out which showed that Tom had been found out: 'Hey, sweetie!' or 'You're a hot bit of property, you are!' But there were other women disguised as she was, and she had Jules and Jim as bodyguards. She carried it off well and was applauded.

Jim was proud for Jules's sake.

Kate was a good person to be about with, unconcerned, offhand, with a gay, sparring style in conversation. She was closer to comedy than Odile, and further from farce. Jim regarded her so much as belonging to Jules that he didn't try to form a clear picture of her. The archaic smile, at once innocent and cruel, appeared on her lips at any time when her face was relaxed: it was natural to her, it expressed the essential Kate.

Jim saw them often; he enjoyed being with them, he enjoyed seeing Jules provided with a woman who was good at receiving his friends. They sang and mimed old French songs together.

They also ran races against one another in the evenings, with a handicap, through the whole length of the Cimetière Montparnasse. Kate won, by cheating at the start.

Jules's two pillows lay side by side on his bed these days, and the bed smelt good.

Jules told Jim that he wanted to marry Kate; and, one fine day, that she had almost said yes. Jim was frightened for them both, he wanted to say, 'Stop! Wait a bit!'

Kate said to him, in front of Jules, 'Mr Jim—'

'No,' Jules interrupted, 'just "Jim".'

'Just Jim,' Kate went on, 'I want to have a talk with you and ask your advice. Will you wait for me tomorrow evening at seven o'clock in the front room at our café?'

Jim consulted Jules with a glance.

'Yes,' said Jules, 'Kate wants to talk to you.'

Did he know what about?

Jim, running, reached the café at four minutes past seven. He was late, as he often was, through being too optimistic. He was displeased with himself, and afraid that he wasn't the first to get there; he looked for Kate but couldn't see her. He sat down, waited for a quarter of an hour, and said to himself, 'A girl like her would be quite capable of coming and looking round, and going off again at a minute past seven because I wasn't there.' The idea ravaged him. He picked up a newspaper automatically and looked at it but put it down again, thinking, 'A woman like her is quite capable of walking quickly through this place without seeing me behind my newspaper, and shooting away again.' He repeated, 'A woman like her – but what *is* she like?' And he began really thinking about Kate; he never had, before. It was half-past seven. He told himself he would wait another quarter of an hour.

He left at ten to eight.

★

Kate, who was even more of an optimist than Jim where time was concerned, had gone to her hairdresser, had a shampoo and wave, and reached the café with all sails set at eight o'clock, intending to have dinner with Jim. She felt disappointed, waited ten minutes and left.

Jules came and told Jim about it the next day.

'If I'd thought there was still any chance she was coming,' said Jim, 'I'd have waited till midnight.'

Jules and Kate set off that same day, to get married in their own country. Jim took them to the train, and gave Kate a funny little pocket-sized folding stool to put under her feet.

If Kate and Jim had met at the café, things might have turned out very differently.

## 2

## *She Jumps into the Seine*

As soon as they were married and had done all the proper family visiting, Jules and Kate came back to Paris. Jim had dinner at their flat. The great Merovingian bed was officially inaugurated. Jules was happy and looked after everything; he was a real man now; Jim saw him masterfully settling questions of laundry, rent, insurance, luggage, and was astounded. But he gradually came to realize that the solutions Jules imposed on these problems were of the same order as the top hat in the stove. Kate was aware of it too, and was undeterred. She said 'Yes' to whatever Jules did, and everything looked all right. Jules would have been hurt by the slightest suggestion that it wasn't.

He was the husband of the blonde woman of his dreams.

Jim took Kate and Jules out to a restaurant on the Quai Voltaire, and gave them a leisurely lunch to celebrate their marriage; everyone chose an individual menu, according to fancy. Kate was wearing a silk dress with stripes of many different colours.

Jules began talking to Jim about literary topics, which interested them both but which could hardly be expected to interest Kate. Jim tried to bring the conversation back in her direction, but in vain; Jules was fairly launched, and to his way of thinking a writer's wife ought to be concerned with these things. Kate, with eyes lowered, was smiling her archaic smile. What was she thinking?

Jules was charming to Jim but was sacrificing Kate quite sense-lessly, for they had already had delightful three-handed conversations. However, instead of ensuring another one, Jules, usually so kind and so modest, was taking the chair and staying in it much longer than one could have expected; it was almost as if he was breaking Kate in. Jim remembered the evening when Magda rebelled; Kate, he thought, would never put up with Jules in this mood, and she was far better armed than Magda. How could Jules be so unimaginative? And how would Kate hit back? And what would happen to their love? Jim was suffering for both of them.

At the end of the long meal, Kate suggested that they go for a walk by the Seine. They went past a former sluice-gate, the Écluse de la Monnaie, and then back along the quay to the Square du Vert-Galant. Jules talked all the way. Suddenly Kate dropped her bag and gloves, gently pushed Jules and Jim aside, and jumped into the Seine.

'Oh, my prophetic soul!' cried a voice in Jim, and at the same time he sent, in thought, an invisible kiss to Kate. Her leap so engraved itself on his imagination that he did a drawing of it next day, although he normally never drew at all. He felt a sudden burst of admiration for her, like a lightning-flash. She, at any rate, wasn't afraid of *doing different*!

Jules was gasping and jittering, as if he was under a shower; he was terrified lest Kate drown. Jim was calm; he had seen how she had let herself fall vertically, quite straight, and he had heard tell of her exploits before. In his mind, he was swimming under water with her and holding his breath with her, making sure of coming to the surface after as long a delay as possible and as far away as possible, so as to give Jules a really good fright.

Kate's straw hat was sailing away downstream on its own, adorned with the multicoloured enamel pin which Jules's mother had given her. Seconds went by. Jules turned his eyes on Jim believing Kate to be lost. Jim motioned to him to wait, and was soon able to point to a fair head emerging thirty yards lower down, a head which veered round and swam towards the bank; the archaic smile was still there, unchanged. She was finding it hard to make her way in; she shouted, 'My dress is bothering me, help me!'

Jim jumped into a boat but it was moored with a padlock and chain. He didn't swim well enough to help a good swimmer like Kate, and he didn't think she really needed help. He ran along, taking off his long mackintosh as he went, and leant over, holding the mackintosh by one sleeve and letting it dangle just above the surface of the water. Kate managed to grab it, and from the top of the sheer quayside he dragged her along against the current, like a fish being drawn to the landing net, until she reached the boat. She hoisted herself aboard, climbed the iron ladder briskly and shook herself between them like a dog.

She was shivering. Jules wrapped her in his coat. Jim ran and got a taxi, pushed the pair of them inside, slammed the door, gave the address to the driver, and went away.

On the next day he found Jules pale, silent, less self-assured and more handsome than before. Kate was like a modest young general who has just returned from his first brilliant coup, his *campagne d'Italie*. Nobody mentioned her plunge.

Jules's mother came to stay with him and Kate, and the three of them toured most of France together.

But it wasn't till much later that Kate and Jules were able to tell Jim how they had got on. Jules's flat was re-let, and the furniture was sent to them in Germany.

They settled in their own country, in a little house by a lake. A daughter was born. Jim was to come on a visit and be her godfather.

Three days before he was due to arrive, the war broke out; it separated them for five years. All either could do was to let the other know, by communicating through neutral countries, that he was still alive. Jules was on the Russian front. There was little likelihood of their encountering one another.

# 3

## 1914: *War* – 1920: *The Chalet*

1919. Peace. They resumed their correspondence. Jules answered all Jim's questions by saying, 'Come and see!'

Another little daughter had been born. Jim wrote to Jules, 'What do you think? Should I get married too? Should I have children?' Jules answered once more, 'Come and judge for yourself.' Kate added a few words of invitation.

Six months later, Jim set out for Jules's country. Seeing Jules again was such a tremendous experience for him that he delayed it; he loitered along the Rhine and stayed in several towns.

The day came. Jim was waiting for Jules in a ground-floor room, and to get there Jules had to cross a wide, grassy square. Jim watched him approaching from a distance, walking dreamily with short, dragging steps, as if he was tired. So he had a wife and two small daughters, he had been right through the war, and now here he was and they were about to meet again – which they might never have done. Jim watched him.

When he was nearly there Jim ran out. They embraced four times.

And their long conversation, which had been merely interrupted, began again. Each found that the other had matured, in his own way, but not changed. They spent two whole days together, sitting at square thick wooden tables and smoking long cigars. They told each other about the war. Jules avoided talking intimately about his family life; Jim had the impression that things weren't going too well.

The next day, Kate was waiting for Jim at the barrier of the little country station, with her two daughters. Jules (perhaps intentionally?) had gone to town to see his publisher.

Kate was in a well-fitting white linen suit; her hair-net was blonde and she wore polished ivory earrings.

Jim gave a start on catching sight of her. Kate had developed into a magnificent woman. Her archaic smile, more clearly defined than before, radiated as ever, and its arrows struck home. Her glance was alive with fantasy and daring which were just held in check. Her bust was proud and graceful, like a ship. Each of her finely shaped hands was holding the hand of a little girl. The older one, Lisbeth, was like Jules, but more Olympian; Martine, the younger, was like Kate.

Kate said: 'Hallo, Jim.'

Her grave voice exactly suited the rest of her. Jim felt it was just as if she had come to meet him at the café, after keeping him waiting a very long time, and that she had dressed specially for him.

She led Jim to their rustic chalet, in the middle of a natural park of pines and sloping meadows. He was to have all his meals with them and sleep at the neighbouring inn.

This was the beginning of an enchanted week for Jim. Every morning Jules brought to his room a flask of coffee, slices of bread and butter, and mild cigars to accompany their conversation. Jules was writing a book, a work of real quality. There was something of the monk about him. He no longer slept in the same room as Kate. She treated him kindly but strictly. Jules let Jim discover the truth, little by little: yes, it was true, the love that had blossomed between them was dying.

Jim was not surprised; he remembered the blunders Jules had made with Magda, and with all the others before her. He could feel that Kate was extremely exacting. He guessed some things and Jules told him others; what they added up to was that Kate was no longer altogether Jules's wife, and that she had had lovers.

Jim was desperately sad; Jules had won for himself the blonde radiance which was the dream of his heart, yet now it was all but denied to him. At the same time, Jim couldn't pass judgement on Kate: mightn't it be that she had leapt into infidelity as she had once leapt into the Seine?

The second week began.

Everything in the house was directed, commandingly, by Kate. She had a governess, Mathilde, an accomplished young woman who enjoyed being her friend. Kate was better than Jules at dealing with his publishers. Jules had definite jobs: he wrote his books, fetched the milk and groceries, went to the post office for the mail, and did it all punctually and cheerfully. The war had severely reduced their income.

Kate made everything into a celebration; the little girls' bath in the evening was a comic ballet which varied from one day to the next, with Jules and Jim as spectators. Every one of their simple meals was a joy. 'Life should be all holidays,' said Kate, and she made it so, for grown-ups and children alike, and yet work was always well done.

She made a cult of her own sleep and always slept as long as she needed, at irregular times, while the household revolved round her independently.

Whenever things were going too well and becoming a habit, she grew discontented; she changed her manner, put on riding boots, picked up a switch as if she had been a lion tamer, and whipped the world with her gestures and expressions.

\*

Her gospel was that the world was rich and that you could cheat a bit sometimes; she always asked God's forgiveness in advance and was confident she'd get it. Calmly, Lisbeth sometimes intimated that she wasn't too sure about that.

There were days when Jim wanted to protect the world against Kate (it had been the same with Odile, but never with Lucie). This was an obsession of his; he had wanted to protect Kate against Jules before their marriage, and during lunch on the day of her plunge into the river. As a rule she was gentle and generous, but if she took it into her head that she wasn't being appreciated she turned aggressive and couldn't be appeased. She swung from one extreme to the other, and these emotional attacks were always sudden.

Jules still wanted her, but suppressed his longing; he knew he had lost her. When she was tormenting him – because she herself was tormented by her inner demon – he was sorry for her. He looked on her as a force of nature which could manifest itself only by cataclysms.

Some undefined threat was hanging over the house.

During the second week, Jim began to understand: the danger was that Kate would leave. She had done it once already, half a year ago, and it had looked as if she didn't mean to return. She had been back only for the last few months. She was full of stress again, Jules could feel that she was working up for something; and he was turning his back on it, as he had done with the crows. He had to admit he no longer had a real wife. That was hard to bear. But then, he wasn't the husband she needed, and she wasn't the woman to bear *that*. He'd got used to her being unfaithful to him occasionally, but not to the idea of her leaving him.

The 'something' took shape, a shape which Jim didn't care for. Albert, the man who was married to Hellas, the first lover of the archaic smile, was on a convalescent holiday in a village near by. Kate had been provocative with him, and said it had been a game to start with – but wasn't everything a game, to her? Albert saw in her the living replica of his statue on the island. Kate had encouraged him and allowed his hopes to rise. He was a head-strong character; he had spoken his mind to Jules and told him he wanted to marry Kate, after she'd got a divorce, and that he would take the girls too.

So there Kate was, ruling radiantly over her home but ready to take wing.

Jim thought: 'She mustn't.'

Jules confided to Jim that Kate, to his knowledge, had had three lovers since they got engaged. One of them had been on the eve of their marriage, a sporting type with whom she had had an affair before; she took him again both as a farewell to her days as a bachelor girl, and in revenge for something that Jules had done without being aware of it.

Three years later, just after the war, she had had a liaison under Jules's eyes with a young friend of his, tall, blond, aristocratic and cultured, whom Jim had known as a boy in Paris and thought very well of. 'Not a bad choice,' thought Jim, 'and they must have had fine times together.'

Kate had dismissed it as 'unimportant'.

Finally, during her recent long absence, she captivated a provincial landowner, who ruled supreme within his own dominions. She had reappeared one fine day, tearful with happiness at being back in her own home, which she set about organizing with zest and love. And there they were.

Jules had all this from Kate herself; she let it out bit by bit, skilfully, leaving plenty to the imagination. And now there was this danger from Albert.

Jim was able to infer that Kate still gave her favours to some extent to Jules, but was drifting further and further away from him. Little by little, Jules was renouncing her, and, with her, everything he had asked of life on earth. That was why he seemed like a monk. He bore Kate no grudge.

Jim wondered if Kate had married Jules for his money. No, he was sure she hadn't; she had been drawn by his mind, his gift of fantasy, his 'Buddhism'. But she needed, in addition to Jules, a male of her own sort.

Jim was far from being sure, but it was possible that she was doing all she could to attract him. There was nothing you could put your finger on. You never knew what she was aiming for until she had got it. Jim and Jules had nicknamed her 'Napoleon', and made up poems about this, which the little girls recited.

One morning, when Jim was about to go to the village, Kate pulled a hairpin out of her hair, gave it to him and asked him to buy her some more like it. On his way, Jim realized that he was carrying the pin between his lips.

Kate could feel that Jules and Jim had been talking about her. She said that she wanted to have a talk with Jim, too, and, in front of Jules, she suggested that she and Jim go for a walk in the woods.

They walked silently at first, along pathways lit by the moon.
'What is it you want to know?' she said.
'Nothing,' said Jim. 'I want to listen to you.'
'So as to pass judgement on me?'
'God forbid!'
'I don't want to tell you anything. I want to ask you questions.'
'All right.'
'My question is: tell me about yourself, Jim.'
'Fair enough, but what shall I tell you?'
'Oh, anything. Do it – oh, *droit devant vous*: just keep straight on.'

★

Jim began: 'Once upon a time, there were two young men . . .' and without naming them he described Jules and himself, their friendship, their life in Paris before the arrival of a certain girl, the impact she made on them, what they thought of her and what came after that – 'Not that one, Jim!' (at this point Jim couldn't help saying his own name); and the consequences, the adventures of the three of them together. For the form's sake she disagreed on one or two details, and added a few herself.

Jim described how they had missed one another at the café.

'What a pity!' he said.

'What a pity!' said Kate.

And he described the three of them as seen through his own eyes . . . He told her what treasures lay hidden in Jules's nature – 'Yes,' she said – and how he had had a presentiment from the beginning that Jules wouldn't be able to keep her.

'Would you have told me all this in the café?'

'Yes.'

'Go on.'

Next came the story of the war and his reunion with Jules, and how resigned Jules had looked; the sudden apparition of Kate, with a daughter on each side of her, at the station barrier; the fortnight of happiness he had just spent with them; all he had seen and all he suspected; Kate's life, or what little he knew of it; and now Albert's proximity, his offer of marriage—

'Are you for Jules and against me?'

'No more than he is himself.'

Jim had been talking for nearly an hour. He hadn't even hidden his passing suspicion that she'd married for money. Now he was silent.

'I'll tell you the whole story over again, just as it happened to *me*,' said Kate.

And from her own angle, going deeper into things than Jim

had done, with a stronger grasp of remembered detail, she began the tale of *Kate and Jules*.

Yes, Jules had dazzled and conquered her by his generosity, his innocence, his absence of self-defence; such a contrast to other men! She thought she could cure him – by joy in love, and by emotional storms which threw him off his bearings; but the storms turned out to be part of his nature. They were happy, yes, but happiness didn't take possession of them and sweep them away. And there they were, face to face, two separate people.

Jules's family was pure torture to Kate. At a reception on the day before the marriage, his mother made a blunder which wounded Kate deeply, and through sheer passivity he virtually took his mother's side. She punished him and wiped out the offence by immediately taking up an old lover of hers, Harold, for a few hours – yes, lover. Thus she was able to marry Jules on level terms; they started with a clean slate. She had never hidden her past love-affairs from him.

The honeymoon round France was just a string of impossible situations. Jules was completely under the thumb of his mother, who was giving them this tour as a present and surrounded them with stupid opulence. Kate gnawed her fist with rage at the thought of having allied herself to their race; she considered herself outraged, and Jules said it was a case of *lèse-majesté*.

Their next phase, by the little lake in Prussia, away from the family, was a mixture of light and shade. They were preoccupied by waiting for their first child. Jules had sent Jim a photo of Kate at this period; she had the expression of an angry lioness. Jim's future goddaughter had a difficult birth, because her parents were not in a state of grace.

War broke out and Jules went to the Eastern Front. He had time to write to her. From a distance she loved him the more and made him a new halo. Their last misunderstanding, the real break between them, came when he was home on leave after two years

of war; she felt she was in the arms of a stranger. He went back
to the front. Their second daughter was born, and the delivery
was an easy one.

'She doesn't look like Jules,' said Jim.

'You may think what you please,' said Kate, 'she's his, all the
same. I told him, "I've given you two daughters. That's enough,
as far as I'm concerned. That chapter's finished. Let's have
separate rooms and I'll have my freedom again."

'A young friend of ours – yours too – Fortunio, was there; free
as air, like me. He was a nice partner; it was like a marvellous
holiday for us both. But he was too young, it didn't amount to
anything.

'I felt the need for some sort of strict, exacting work, close to
the soil. I took a job on a farming estate in the North. I began at
the bottom, working with the farm-girls. The water in the jug
on my washstand was frozen every morning. I learnt about arable
farming and looking after stock. It was a fine life.

'My eye was caught by the master, a man in his prime, feared
by everyone, and his eye was caught by me.

'My life changed. He took me out shooting boar and deer, and
I learnt to swear like him at lazy keepers or beaters; I was still
working, but higher up. That was a fine life, too. I might almost
have gone on with it – but one day I felt stifled, by so much para-
phernalia. To my surprise I missed Jules's calm indulgence and
my daughters pulled me like a magnet. I was on the wrong track.
I went home.

'I've only been back three months. Jules is finished for me, as
a husband. Don't be sorry on his account. I allow him some liber-
ties now and then, and it's enough for him.

'What next? Well, there's Albert, not far from where we are
now. He told me about that Greek statue you three were in love
with. I've been flirting with him. There are some odd things about
him, but he's got natural authority; there's none of that in

Fortunio, or Jules. He wants me to leave Jules and get married to him. He would take the two daughters as well as their mother. I feel very friendly towards him, but that's all so far. I shall see.

'You've listened to me very nicely. I've talked more than you did. It's dawn now. I don't pretend to have told you everything, but then neither did you. I expect you think I've had other lovers. Well, that's my business. I've told you as much as you told me, and no more. Let's get back.'

There was not much further to go to the villa. Kate *must* stay! To what extent was Jim about to act for Jules's sake, and to what extent for his own? That was something he would never know. He was putting off the critical moment. As they drew level with the last tree in the clump separating them from the house, only twenty yards from where Jules lay sleeping, he put his hands on Kate's shoulders and let his face approach hers a little. They gazed at one another. What was going to happen? There was a lengthy pause. Kate suddenly came very close and let her cheek and her top lip gently graze his mouth. He felt an inexpressible sweetness go through him. He lifted his hands from Kate's shoulders and she ran to the house.

# 4

## Albert – the Camp Fire

Albert was coming to lunch the day after next.

Jim told Jules all about his walk with Kate, including the final gesture. Jules listened without a word: he was like a spectator at billiards, watching the balls roll. Jim felt nevertheless that Jules was beginning to side with him against Albert.

Albert was correct and ordinary. Kate amused herself by teasing each of the three men in turn, paying them compliments which sounded *naïf*, but weren't. Nobody answered. Her smile held the reins of this unruly team. At her ease, mistress at her own table, she directed the conversation and showed a touch of tyranny in doing so; it was her turn to be loquacious now. Being a different person with each of the three, she couldn't strike the right note with them all there at once. She could feel that she wasn't quite coming off, was angry with them for it, and forced the pace.

She lit up their three fat cigars for them in her own mouth, but they all felt this as a lack of tact, a kind of promiscuity. Jim wanted to throw away his cigar and walk out; but he stayed because he wanted to fall out of love with her.

She put on her riding boots and picked up her switch, playing the part of an animal-tamer on a fairground. Animals? The men were the animals. She exhibited them to themselves.

Thought Jim, 'A cock looks silly in the middle of his hens. And a hen looks just as silly with three cocks – unless they fight to the death for her. Maybe that's what Kate wants.'

A long walk together dissipated the ill-humour of all four. They went as far as the camp of some show-people who ran a little wandering circus. One of the wagons, clean and gay, held a swarm of seven children, ranging from one to twelve years old, healthy and merry like their parents.

'That's real riches, real happiness!' said Kate, with emotion. She gave them some sweets and all the money in her bag. Jim fell under her spell again.

She bestowed her graciousness on each in turn. With Albert it was on account of a collection of stones in a glass case; she and he had such a collection when they were at school together; they bandied strange geological names, and Jim was jealous.

At the circus performance, watching the children doing their turns as clowns and acrobats, Kate rediscovered the atmosphere of her own enchanted childhood.

When Albert had gone they discussed him. Jules, who was happy and hilarious, asked Kate what she had done to charm him, and Kate acted a caricature of herself describing, almost in good faith, what an unhappy life she had at home. Jules, Jim and Mathilde laughed till the tears ran down their cheeks. The danger of her going off with Albert seemed to have been averted for the moment, but not that of a short adventure. Everyone was on Jim's side.

'But,' Jules told Jim, 'Kate never lets go of anything, once she's had a hold of it.'

Jim, who was curious, gently and kindly pointed out certain ways in which Kate's and Jules's versions of their story didn't tally; he asked them to give him a completer picture. So it was agreed that they should go for a long walk, during which Kate and Jules would take up the story alternately.

After a somersaulting competition on the grass with the little girls, they set out in the direction of a country inn, some six or seven miles away. Jules, at Kate's request, spoke first. He did it with his usual humour and modesty, making them laugh with his depiction of himself falling in love with Kate. All this opening passage went well, and Jim was looking forward to an entertaining joust between these two master story-tellers. But tension filled the air when Jules got as far as the marriage and his family, and he gave a description of Kate's jump into the Seine with which neither she nor Jim agreed; he portrayed it as a mere impulse on Kate's part and not as a riposte which he had forced her to make. Next came their journey round France with Jules's mother. Kate was indignant, interrupted him and became angry. It had been agreed beforehand that this comparison of memories should be made without quarrelling, but Kate was re-living the indignities she had been made to suffer. She had made no sign at the time, and Jules had been able to convince himself that she was satisfied; but in fact the debt had been piling up inside her. It was disastrously clear that Jules still hadn't understood.

Despair and rage descended on her like a black cloud. It was the first time Jim had seen her ravaged like this.

Soon she was including Jim in her contempt, as well as Jules. She was almost at the pitch of saying, 'Men . . .' as Jules in days gone by used to say, 'Women . . .' Her outburst gave Jim an insight into Jules's emotional crises. He said to himself, 'We all have our crises, in our different ways, and they are always unconscious. What sort of crises do I have?'

It was by moments like these that Kate paid for her buoyant happiness, her conception of life as an endless holiday, the joy she radiated round her – and she made other people pay too.

Dinner went badly, and the walk home was bitter and wretched.

Kate spent the next day in her room.

But on the day after that the sky was blue again.

They held a competition in the garden, with a toy gun and little rubber darts. They fired at balloons thrown up into the air. Kate was the winner. After that they shot at a target and Kate discovered that Jim pulled an odd face when he was aiming. She fetched a mirror, to show him, but he couldn't make the face and look at it at the same time. She got him to make it again when they had finished shooting, saying, 'Aim at me!' The little girls aimed at him meanwhile, imitating his face.

Jim taught everyone how to handle a great bow. The copper-tipped arrow sped up so high towards the sun that they lost sight of it. They were frightened lest it come down on someone's head, and during its descent they shut their eyes and held each other's hands.

Jim came back from an expedition one day with a boomerang of some hardwood or other, in the shape of a bent elbow. After a few trials the weapon soared away from them against the wind, described a circle and stuck itself upright in the turf, just beside Lisbeth. They gave up throwing it after that.

Life really was a holiday.

On one occasion Jim was left looking after Martine, on the bank of the big mere. She was three, and because it was hot she was wearing her pyjamas. She cast a glance at Jim, as much as to say, 'You understand me, you do,' stepped out of her pyjama-trousers and walked into the water. She stopped for a moment and took off the jacket, throwing it to Jim in a way which was just like her mother's. He watched this naked child advancing confidently, with short steps, towards the middle of the mere; the water came up to her shoulders before she turned. For the first time he was directly aware that he wanted a child by Kate.

*

He was working alone in the dining-room. A noise behind him made him start: it was Lisbeth, whom he had taught to shoot; she had shot an arrow at the window-pane. Jim explained gently that she might have broken the glass and that she mustn't shoot at the window. She listened to him, her eyes candid, seeming to have taken it in. But her arrow struck the window three times more, and Jim gave her three different explanations of why she oughtn't to do it. Kate arrived, looked at her daughter with a smile and said, 'No.' And that was that. Jim was astonished that he hadn't got it across to her himself. Kate told him:

'I'm sure she'd made up some wonderful drama, in which it was her duty to shoot at the window.'

Kate, Annie, her plump malicious cousin, her friend Rachel, the tall brunette who had been one of the trio in Paris, Jules and Jim, set out with rucksacks into the woods, had supper there and went for a long walk by moonlight. The night was cool and dewy. Kate, as the leader, halted and made a camp fire; the others all helped. Tall flames rose, and Kate said, 'Let's each throw something into the fire, as a sacrifice, and make a wish.' She herself threw in a silk scarf, which burnt in the air, without having time to fall. The only thing Jim had worth sacrificing was his knife; he threw in a notebook. His wish was connected with Kate.

Rachel, who was hostile to Jim, kept trying to get a word alone with Kate. Kate and her cousin had decided to shock Rachel; they told each other fearful stories whose morality was decidedly unusual, and Rachel got really cross. Jules was collapsing with laughter and had to pretend to have a cough. He had had a headache that evening and had taken aspirin, and was absent-minded and fey at times as a result.

Kate challenged her cousin to a wrestling-match with the palms of the hands held flat, a clowning performance full of impossible entanglements which Rachel admiringly applauded. Then Kate challenged Jim. They rolled over and over on the grass and dead leaves, grunting and gasping and nearly rolling into the fire. Jim had Kate in his arms and was in no hurry to end the game. Rachel said afterwards that perhaps they had been doing something other than wrestling.

They walked on for a long time and came in the pitch darkness to a grassy sward on the edge of a lake that Kate knew well. She left the others, and it wasn't long before they heard the splash as she dived. She stayed in the water long enough to scare Jules. She was deceiving her men with the water-gods.

She reappeared out of the darkness, delighted and shivering; her cousin and Rachel rubbed her with a rough towel which she had brought along for this very purpose.

The sun rose. A travelling pedlar sold them schnapps. A green-grocer's shop stall opened, and Jules went to buy fruit for them all. As he was tired, and also because of the aspirin, he showed the woman what fruit he wanted by pointing with his forefingers from the level of his thighs, not bothering to raise his arms; and rolling his head about so as to point with his nose as well. He was muttering away at the same time, addressing now the shop-woman, now himself and now the Almighty, all in the same tone of voice. The others were watching him from behind a quite inadequate bush, trying to stifle their laughter. When, laden with fruit, he rejoined them, they all kissed him, and that woke him up for a moment.

In the dewy undergrowth, they came across some roe-deer; and they did not get back to the chalet, to sleep, till it was after-noon.

## 5

## *Kate and Jim – Annie*

Late one evening, Kate asked Jim to go to the inn and fetch a
book for her. When he came back everyone else was in bed. Kate
met him in the big rustic dining-room, which smelt pleasantly
of polished wood.

She was in white pyjamas and had powdered her smooth face.
He had been longing for her all day.

She was in his arms now, sitting on his knees, and her voice was
deep. This was their first kiss, and it lasted the rest of the night.
They didn't talk; they let their intimacy take hold of them and
bring them closer and closer together. She was revealing herself
to him in all her splendour. Towards dawn, they became one.
Kate's expression was full of an incredible jubilation and curiosity.
This perfect union, and the archaic smile, more accentuated now
– Jim was irresistibly drawn. When he got up to go he was a man
in chains. Other women had ceased to exist for him.

Their happiness spread through the whole house. Mathilde, who
had always been afraid of Albert, was confident now: 'At last!'
she said.

The little girls felt gay, without knowing why.

Jules never reminded Jim of his 'Not that one!' Tacitly, he gave
them his blessing.

He was frightened by the speed at which their love got under
way. 'Look out, Jim!' he said '– for her sake and your own.'

'That's all very well,' thought Jim, 'but what are we supposed to be looking out for?'

Kate rearranged the rooms, squashing people up a bit, and asked Jim to come and live at the chalet. He had his own little bedroom, but he slept with Kate. They hadn't an instant of life to lose.

Kate had a big square room with a double bed, and an enormous, timber-built terrace-balcony with a balustrade of boards decorated with carvings, where no one could see them.

During the day Kate, Jules and Jim often sat there, in the sun or the shade according to the weather. They had baths out there, making plenty of froth with the soap and splashing about. Kate's ideas on the matter were Japanese: the nude is erotic only when it means to be. She had her bath under their eyes, taking her time; then it was Jim's turn and then Jules's, the conversation continuing meanwhile. It was a counterpoint of bodies. Jules and Jim were living with their Greek statue; the stone goddess had come to life, and they were grateful to her.

'We must begin again at the beginning,' said Kate, 'and re-discover the rules, taking risks and paying on the nail.' This was one of the fundamental articles of her credo, which Jim shared and which united them. Jules was neither for nor against; he was a benevolent spectator, formulating and classifying the discoveries of the other two as they made them. It amused him sometimes to bring out an old Greek or Chinese text which said the same thing as they did. 'That may be,' said Kate, 'but people had forgotten it.'

One hot day, when they had been pouring pitchers of cold water over one another, Kate decided to seduce Jules. He was in his own corner of the balcony, on his raffia mattress; she went over, sat on his knees, pushed him on to his back and lay on top of him. 'No, no,' said Jules. 'Yes, yes!' said Kate. It became clear to

Jim, who was only a few yards away in the other corner, that she was giving him enormous pleasure. Jim wasn't watching them; he approved of Kate's action and was glad for Jules. He was wondering, 'Would I be feeling the same if I thought they were going all the way?'

There was a silence. Kate and Jules began talking again, in low voices. Jules was looking ashamed but pleased.

A little later, Kate made a set at Jim. Looking down into the dark profundities of her eyes, Jim was astonished to see no flicker of response to his own unrestricted outpouring of love.

The day passed off quietly; Kate didn't turn against either of them. She was thinking, 'Jim didn't try and stop me. He trusts me, he's not jealous of the concessions I make to Jules.'

Kate did not indulge again in such a feast – or experiment, whichever it was for her.

A month earlier, before his arrival at the chalet, Jim had spent a couple of days in town on a visit to Annie, Kate's cousin; she had lent him her studio. Jim was free then, and had flirted with Annie. She had told him how she was in love with a painter with a pagan profile like the face on a medallion, and had introduced him to Jim. This had not deterred Jim and herself from exchanging a good many kisses.

During one of his visits to town since then, Jim had seen her again and danced with her, and in saying good-bye had playfully kissed a curl of her hair. This happened in front of Rachel, who at once came and told Kate and Mathilde, and had a good deal to say about it.

Kate instantly thought the worst. Jim had had an affair with Annie, and had now started it up again!

She said nothing and invited Annie to stay. Annie, at her ease, shared their games in the park. Jim was in Kate's pocket. But Mathilde, outraged by the tale of Jim's betrayal of Kate with Annie, thought she saw Jim and Annie kissing on the sly. And that evening, during pencil-and-paper games with the little girls, Annie appeared to fall into a 'Freudian trap' by writing down something oddly unsuitable.

Kate remained impassive. She invited Jim to come for a stroll in the park. She had swathed herself in a shining snowy scarf, with a turban of the same material. She had suddenly become cold and sarcastic. Jim questioned her but got nowhere. At last she said:

'I've decided to be Albert's mistress tomorrow. I've sent for him already.'

Jim was struck down in the midst of his happiness. She wouldn't give any explanation; but he persisted desperately, bit by bit pieced together the business of Annie and Rachel and at last saw what had happened. He admitted that he had flirted briefly with Annie a month ago – but since falling in love with Kate he no longer had a thought for anyone else; surely that was obvious? But Kate was stony and unattainable; he wasn't even sure she was listening. It took him two hours' hard work, including the offer of a joint visit to Annie, to get Kate to postpone her gesture. She accepted the offer and, for the first time, sent him to his own room after he had said good night to her.

They took the first train in the morning. Kate asked Annie to put them up; she also asked her to invite her painter-friend to come in and organized a sort of miniature masked ball for the four of them, with disguises and a buffet and a gramophone, and she behaved by turns as guest and as Grand Inquisitor. She set about charming the painter, leaving Annie and Jim a free hand. They sensed the pitfall. Annie was frightened by the havoc Kate could cause in her life. The painter left in the small hours; Kate, almost pacified, jumped into Jim's bed and arms, giving Annie permission to make drawings of them – she wanted to see from Annie's expression whether she was in love with Jim after all, and also whether Jim would be embarrassed by Annie's presence. He wasn't. They forgot Annie. She left some epic drawings pinned on the wall.

Jim felt their love catch fire again, and all his zest for living came back. He went off to spend five days with some eminent compatriots of Kate's; he was still full of her all the time he was with them, and because of her he was quicker to understand and appreciate them. On the fourth day he got an ambiguous letter from her. She didn't like absences, and he hurried back.

Kate had gone on a walking-trip for two days in the mountains, alone, and had afterwards made an hour-by-hour record of her experiences. Her state of bliss gave way by degrees to renewed doubts. When all was said, there had been something, before she came into it, between Annie and Jim. No man who belonged to Kate was allowed to be suspect. If there was any doubt at all about him, he must be punished. Besides, this man Jim mustn't get too sure of himself. She must cancel out the situation in her own way; then they could start again with a clean page.

She summoned Albert on the fourth day, spent several hours with him, gave him plenty of passionate caresses (later described in her diary), and sent him away full of hope.

In her mind, each lover was a separate world, and what happened in one world was no concern of the others. But this didn't prevent her from being jealous herself.

She had once taken her elder daughter, who was unwell, to see a doctor, and had said:

'This is my only daughter, Doctor.'

The child was surprised and mentioned her younger sister.

'Well?' said the doctor.

'The other one's my second only daughter,' said Kate.

Her attitude to love was just the same.

★

Jim came back, on fire for her, and it seemed to him that his love was met with love. At the same time he could sense something strange in the atmosphere, and something like embarrassment in Jules. He asked Kate. She spent several days distilling the poison in her heart, before telling him what she had done with Albert.

Jim recognized the delayed-action method which she had used on Jules. To him, her action was just a senseless piece of destructiveness.

Jules and Mathilde, who had stopped being afraid of trouble from Albert since Jim had come, had started worrying again.

Jules told Kate.

'He that killeth with the sword must be killed with the sword.'

She looked at him triumphantly:

'If I'm the least bit doubtful,' she said, 'I always do more than can possibly have been done to me.'

Jim wanted to leave. But his straightforward grief won Kate over completely, and she succeeded in making him stay. He understood eventually that her aim had been to *do justice*; maybe it was only an obsession of hers, but still, it was something which was necessary to her.

'All right,' he said, 'let's make a fresh start.'

They began a new honeymoon, and so did the whole house.

One evening she read them her favourite passage in Kleist's *Penthesilea*, in which the frenzied Amazonian queen murders Achilles. The hero is unarmed and frantic with desire for her.

'Why does she kill him?' said Jim. 'Why is she armed when he isn't? Can't she get the better of him any other way? And why get the better of him at all, if they're in love? By killing him, she proves her inferiority. Or does she kill herself after?'

Kate answered:

'Is there anything more beautiful than the red blood of the

one who loves you?' She added, 'I'm in the very middle of your own red heart, Jim, and I want to drink and drink and drink.'

Jules had once said:

'An archaic smile feeds on milk – and blood.'

Kate's lips were made for both.

# 6

## The Locomotive-In Town

In the middle of this honeymoon Kate decided on a change of setting. She wanted to leave the chalet, go and live in town alone with Jim, and practise dancing in the afternoons and work up a variety act.

They went down to the station with Jules and Mathilde, dumped their cases on the platform and waited for the train. Night was falling. Kate was amusing herself by balancing on the gleaming rail. The locomotive's great fiery eyes swung into view on a bend in the line, and got larger and larger. Kate, on the rail, walked towards them. Jules was terrified, these acrobatics of hers were more than he could bear; he was shouting, 'Kate, Kate, you're crazy! Stop! Kate, please stop!'

Kate became twice as daring and started doing dance-steps. The locomotive's headlights were looming closer.

Jim said to Jules, in a low voice:

'Shut up, Jules, you're only making her worse, she loves it when you're frightened.'

The train was slowing down now, coming into the station. Jim went and stood by the cases, watching Kate. At the last moment she jumped lightly aside, out of the glare of the headlights. Fine! Jim stooped, picked up the cases and ran towards the front of the train; he had seen some room there. It was almost too dark to distinguish anything. He stumbled into a dark bulk which was lying on the ground, jumped over it and almost fell. He turned and peered down; it was a woman's body. People were crowding round. He was about to go on towards the front of the train and join Kate when someone came up with a lantern, and Jim recognized Jules crouching over the body. The woman on the ground was Kate.

He could see arms lifting her to her feet, and she stood upright, swaying. Jim felt her with his hands and moved her limbs; there didn't seem to be anything broken. She murmured, 'It's my head. At the back.' Jim touched it and found blood on his hand. She had a scalp wound.

The locomotive was wider than Kate had realized, dazzled as she was by its lights, and it had just touched her, brushing her aside. She walked three steps.

'Are we going just the same, Kate?' said Jim.

'Yes,' said Kate.

There was still time. Half supporting, half pushing her, Jim got to the front coach and hoisted her up like a parcel, then grabbed the cases as Jules and Mathilde reached them up to him. The train had just started. The coach was full but people made room for Kate. She had a brief faint. Then Jim had to leave her and stand on the smoky observation-platform, which was crammed with men.

Jim and Jules were never able to reconstruct Kate's precise movements before to the moment of impact. And she herself could remember nothing.

They settled in a small *pension*. They had two narrow beds, which they pulled together to make one. Kate had a large bruise on one thigh, a cut on the head and a number of grazes, and was stiff and sore all over. Jim was wedded to her convalescence. During the first few days they didn't get up. Kate recovered, and did drawings for him of visions which she had had when she was still running a temperature.

'If you tidied up these drawings and wrote down the things you've just been telling me,' said Jim, 'any advanced review would publish them.'

'Are you sure, Jim?'

'Quite sure.'

She began drawing again, propped up with her back against Jim; she didn't like him to be away from her, and he didn't like it either. Sometimes he helped her by just holding her feet. As soon as the drawings and letterpress were finished they sent them off.

'But if they're a success,' said Kate, 'I shall want to do more. And then it'll turn into a professional job, just as it is for Jules. And I don't want a job!'

'Success has its points, though,' said Jim. 'Besides, you won't have to draw unless you want to.'

Kate, feeling that she must get out of their hothouse of love and draw a breath of fresh air – feeling, indeed, that she and Jim would die of it if she didn't – revived her idea of getting up a dance-number. She rented a studio nearby and went there by herself in the afternoons. Jim trusted her completely and never went with her. But was she really by herself? Jim wondered, after a while. In any case, she was giving herself to him so absolutely in every way that nothing else could mean much to her. To Jim, their love was something immense, a Mont Blanc, and at this juncture he couldn't be bothered about whatever might be lurking in the valleys.

Kate was making notes for a theory of physical love, and showing them to friends – women, not men. She and Jim frequently saw Annie, without ill-feeling on either side.

A letter, with the name and emblem of the review on the envelope, arrived for Kate.

Her drawings were to appear in the next issue, and the editor wanted more!

'There, you see, Jim!' said Kate, alarmed and overjoyed.

\*

At noon one day, Kate, with a pail in her hand, went into the passage which led past their room. She was dressed in a red silk pyjama jacket, without the trousers.

'You'll meet someone!' Jim shouted.

'Not likely at this time of day,' she said, 'besides, it's a tradition in my family to take risks of this kind.'

They went to a music-hall show. In one of the acts, a tramp wanted to steal a bicycle which had been left against a tree. He kept taking off his yellow choker and putting it on again, so as to keep his hands busy and resist temptation. And in the end he stole it just the same. It was perfect. They tried, unsuccessfully, to meet him at the stage door.

Jim loved the full moon, but Kate didn't. 'Love and the moon,' she said, 'so obvious and banal!' Probably moonlight had bad associations for her.

They wandered among the alleys and sidestreets of the city; one of their pleasures was to talk to some craftsman or other, in the back shop.

They worked themselves up over fantastic plans, and what they thought were new ideas, for making plenty of money while still having plenty of time to themselves. One of the incidental objects was to be able to give presents to Jules, but it was difficult to know what to give him, because there was nothing he wanted.

They felt reverent towards everything.

They went into a church one day. Kate was a Protestant, Jim a Catholic. Like the crowd, they knelt and waited. Communion was about to begin; two long lines of nuns, with eyes lowered and hands clasped before them, advanced towards the communion table; three of them, young, white-habited, were particularly beautiful. To Jim's surprise Kate got up and joined them, copying their attitudes and taking communion with them, after a sideways glance to find out how they received the host. Sacrilege on her part? No, Kate was acting quite spontaneously; she would have done the same in any religious ceremony, in any part of the world. She came back and meditated with the sisters for a while, and her face when she raised it at the end was peaceful.

There was still a week left of their stay when Kate had a dramatic letter from Rachel: 'You must choose: it's Jim or your children.'

'Quite wrong,' said Jim: 'it's Jim *and* your children.'

'Well,' said Kate decisively, 'when you've come to the end of something you should always anticipate and cut it short. Let's throw away this last week.' And she felt a powerful longing, which was shared by Jim, to see her daughters again, and Jules and Mathilde and the chalet. They set out next day.

Jules was waiting for them on the platform of the little station, standing where Kate had fallen. She jumped down while the train was still in motion, ran to him, folded him in her arms and gave him a long kiss. 'Tell me,' she said '– tell me all the wonderful things which have been happening here too.' Jules, smiling, began describing the uneventful life they had been leading 'till mummy comes back'.

When they got outside the station Jules wanted to go off and fetch the milk and though she tried to stop him he insisted. He disappeared waving to them.

'That's just like Jules,' she said, 'I come back, I kiss him, I'm happy, and he goes to fetch the milk!'

'He'll be back in five minutes,' said Jim.

'Yes, but my happiness has been cut off short.'

The little girls and Mathilde gave Kate an adoring welcome, some of whose reflected glory fell on Jim.

On a very hot day the three of them made a pilgrimage on foot to an enormous, massive monastery, deep in a long, lush, damp valley. There was complete harmony between them. They liked the big, white, ascetic refectory and the fresh, simple food. They visited the impressive stockyard and buildings, many of whose inmates were prizewinners at shows. Kate made expert comments; she was proud of having been a farm-hand for a few weeks and delighted to explain all they saw. All three understood the attraction of the soil, but it made Jules and Jim feel quite inadequate and useless. Kate would have liked to buy a big farm, but Jules's capital had already depreciated too much.

They came back along a stream which was turbulent in parts; in one place there was a waterfall. They decided that the mass of falling water was like Kate, the uneven surges just below were like Jim, and the succeeding calm stretch was like Jules.

They came on long tracts which the stream had left bare, wonderful banks of sand strewn with white stones. Throwing stones was one of Jim's pleasures, and here there was plenty of good ammunition. He threw high, and sent another stone to meet it while the first was still on the way down. Sometimes the two collided in the air and shivered into pieces. Kate made him go on till he was tired out. She and Jules learnt how to play ducks and drakes. The sky seemed very near.

October came. There was no talk of Albert now. They went through a gentle, uneventful phase, with the little girls and Mathilde.

Kate and Jim were both active, and liked showing their prowess. One day, getting out of a field just at the moment when a group of peasants were approaching, the two of them vaulted over a gate. It ought to have looked very graceful, but the gate was rotten and broke under their hands; they rolled together in the grass, and the peasants went on without a glance.

November. Jim had to go back to Paris; both his mother and his work were there. Perhaps he ought never to have gone? In Kate's eyes, his doing so relegated their love to the domain of the relative, and that was something she couldn't tolerate. Jim would be back in the spring; but, for a woman like Kate, what a lot of water would have gone under the bridge by then!

Once again she accompanied him to town. They had often boarded this smoky little train together. They were holding hands; she had taken off her gloves and one of them lay inside out on her lap, looking like a heart with the aorta severed.

'Look at my heart on your knees,' said Jim.

They stayed in town and Jim kept putting off his departure day after day. Its imminence made them thrust the limitations of their lives away from themselves; they drew their breath precariously, as if held in thrall by a spell. One afternoon they telephoned Jules together, in a little upholstered cubicle in a brasserie. Jim was standing behind Kate, his body just touching her back in the half-light; he breathed her aroma and he almost fainted.

They thought of death as the fruition of love, something they would attain together; any time, perhaps even tomorrow.

Kate, at lunch with a group of friends, introduced Jim to the athletic Harold, who had been her lover before she was engaged, and again on the day before her marriage. Jim felt no distrust towards Harold; it seemed to him that Kate was as invulnerable as himself. Harold was well dressed, well built and a good rider, and had just won a race. He also went in for boxing, like Jim. He was casual and intelligent, using the whip of conversation to drive the little group of women at table – with the exception of Kate – as an Eskimo uses a whip to drive his sledge-dogs.

Jim couldn't imagine there had ever been any real love between Harold and Kate, she was of too fine a stamp, too exacting, for Harold to move her much.

Jim went alone to a film which Kate had seen already, and which he was thinking of buying; Kate went shopping with Harold in the meantime. Jim joined them afterwards and they had tea. Harold overflowed with self-confidence; he talked very fast and jerkily to Kate, but in a slightly hoarse voice which was more effective than anything else in keeping Jim reassured. The only common ground which he and Harold found between them was their liking for certain painters.

Their last night came. Kate sat, like Venus on a shell, in the big handbasin in their bedroom. The separation would have been heart-breaking for Jim if he hadn't known that they'd be together again soon, unchanged, intact.

When the train went out they waved to each other for a long time, gently.

Jules had laid a kind of blessing on them and embraced Jim, who committed Kate into his hands.

For Kate and Jim wanted to marry and have children.

# 7

## *Gilberte – Albert – Fortunio*

So Jim came back to Paris. For years he had had a girl there, Gilberte, whom he saw at intervals; it was inclination, not passion, a lightweight love which he hardly noticed. 'But that is another story.' As compared with the frozen mountains, the burning plains, the thunderstorms and typhoons of Kate's love, Gilberte presented a level, delicate landscape with a temperate climate, in which the light of the sky was the sum total of events. Jim had never been deprived of her and had never felt that she made any demand on him.

Gilberte and Jim had met soon after they were both twenty. They were drawn to each other's characters; it was friendship *plus* attraction. They had concluded a tacit alliance against passion. They loved each other tactfully, in secret, without bringing their friends, their interests or any material question into it; they made love in a tiny flat, high up, with an enormous view, which Jim had rented for them and at which they met for a whole day every week. As they saw each other so little, their love consisted only of what was best and most disinterested in themselves. They had hardly any desire to meet more often; they led separate lives. Once a year they spent a week in the country. Jim had never visited Gilberte at her home, nor had Gilberte ever been to Jim's regular flat. Both had travelled, on their own, in Jim's case sometimes for several years on end; but they had always joined forces again, without being tied to each other in any way.

Ten years went by as lightly as a breath. Gilberte, one day, mentioned her mother, whom she had lost at the age of five; she showed Jim a photo of herself at the orphan school to which she had been sent until an aunt could come and collect her. In this photo Gilberte, surrounded by her companions, looked so straightforward, trusting and helpless that Jim, without realizing it, had adopted that little girl, for ever.

A few years later, Jim asked her if she wouldn't like to marry him. They studied the question deliberately. They went to see a doctor specializing in eugenics; he told them their children wouldn't be strong. In addition, they would have had to share Jim's mother's flat for a while, which alarmed Gilberte. They decided to make no change.

Jim had, however, said to her, 'If you like, we'll live together when we're old.'

And Gilberte had said to Jim, 'If ever you want to have a wife and family, you can trust me to keep out of the way.'

In seventeen years Jim hadn't had a single thing with which to reproach Gilberte. He felt quite free to marry, but not to abandon all responsibility for Gilberte. Two of the qualities she had come to personify, in his view of life, were *honour* and *moderation*. Gilberte was not oblivious to the fact that he had adventures during his lengthy travels abroad; but he always came back to her. Jim had no idea whether she was faithful to him, but as time went on it seemed more and more probable that she was.

He couldn't leave her, any more than Kate could leave Jules. Neither Gilberte nor Jules must get hurt. In their different ways they were both fruit produced by the tree of the past, a counterpart and counterpoise to each other. Kate and Jim must be kind to them. Perhaps, some day, Gilberte would accept what Jules accepted already? Perhaps the four of them would be able to live together, with the two little girls and the children who would be born in the years to come, in one big country house, where everyone could work in his own way? That was Jim's dream.

Given that there were four people variously joined together by love, was there any reason why the result should be discord? Kate wasn't betraying Jim by being kind to Jules. Jim wasn't betraying Kate by remaining fond of Gilberte. He felt no conflict inside him between them; they appealed to different regions of his heart. How he longed that Kate, too, would never feel any conflict in herself between him and Jules; and that Kate and Gilberte would never be enemies!

Jim had always told Gilberte about the women he had made love to while he was living abroad, and he had always described her to them in a way that won their respect. He had portrayed her to Kate on the morning after their long walk. Kate had been a bit scornful about their long, uneventful friendship, which she called 'sensible' and 'resigned'. No more damning words existed in Kate's vocabulary.

Jim put forward an axiom: 'Jules equals Gilberte.' In time he was to discover that Kate had adopted a different one: 'Gilberte does not equal Jules.'

Gilberte occupied on the fringe of Jim's life a position whose importance he had never clearly defined, and he didn't think his passion for Kate would give Gilberte any permanent distress.

Kate and Jim decided, by correspondence, to hurry their marriage along so that they could start having children straight away. Jules was in perfect agreement and was ready to do whatever was necessary for a quick divorce. This much settled, Jim plucked up his courage, or what he mistook for his courage, and spoke to Gilberte. He told her briefly about Kate, their wish for children and marriage, and Jules's acquiescence. Gilberte already knew Jules pretty well from Jim's description, without having met him.

Gilberte listened to Jim, sitting up very straight, without flinching. When he had finished she said:

'I'm giving you my consent now, quickly, while I've still got the willpower to do it.'

She turned for a moment, leaning her breasts against the back of the couch; then she got up and went out of the room.

'Don't cause suffering, Jim,' Lucie had said.

Jim suddenly felt, 'I've committed a murder.' But an hour later he was telling himself hopefully, 'She'll get used to it.'

While in Paris he made a few brief farewells.

Kate spent the winter with Jules in their snow-covered chalet. She was Jim's fiancée now, being looked after by Jules. She asked Jules every day, 'Do you think Jim loves me?'

As she had promised, Kate was writing the story of their lives during the previous summer; depicting, with surprising intensity, everything which had happened both in and around her, and everything she had done – not forgetting Albert. Jules felt that the account gave him the key to the gales and tidal waves of Kate's temperament, and he encouraged her to go on.

March came. Jim made preparations for earning his living in Kate's country. He translated a play which was running successfully there, and agreed to go and stay for a fortnight with the author, to put the final polish on his translation.

In addition he was feeling a need to delay the moment, a need to prepare for it, just as he had before his reunion with Jules; it suited him very well to play truant in rural surroundings for a little while.

It seemed to Kate that Jim was in no hurry to see her again.

Jim, with his playwright, was passing through Kate's home town. He sent word, and she and Jules came to drink tea with them in Jim's hotel.

She had got slightly plumper; the result of sitting so much in her room, writing. It almost made her blush to come visiting as a bride-to-be, escorted by Jules (like a heifer being taken to the bull, she said later). Jim wasn't her Jim: he was receiving her in a public place, and he had hired out his time, like a servant, to a third party who would soon be taking him away again. She was in the full bloom of her beauty – and thought she was less beautiful than before. Jules felt intuitively that this meeting was ill-omened. Jim explained that he was working for Kate. But did that mean anything to her at all? He ought to have dropped everything and come straight to the real presence that was Kate.

She asked him a few questions about his good-byes in Paris, and he gave what he thought were satisfactory answers.

The sight of Kate gripped his heart. He would have liked to stay with her and never leave her – but there was no getting out of it, he had to go.

At last, three weeks later, he came back to the chalet. Kate wasn't there. She had only just gone away – on business, like Jim – and was staying with her sister in the capital. Jim was disappointed but thought it quite normal. Jules didn't. When Kate went off on her own it was always dangerous.

Jules described how Kate had sat writing her diary. He had never known her do that before. She had been hurt to discover, when they had tea together in the hotel, that Jim had written a mass of notes about their life together but hadn't made his notes into a book.

Her letters were short, she was putting off her return and talking of business matters, as Jim had done.

Jules and Jim were completely alone in the chalet, alone with their leisure, their peaceful life and their inexhaustible conversation. A peasant woman came in and did a little summary housework. Jules was translating a book by Jim; he also did the cooking, with his pipe in his mouth, and made potato-cakes while Jim read aloud. They went for slow, lazy walks together.

The divorce had been set in motion. Jules was afraid of something, but Jim couldn't discover what. They wrote to Kate, saying that everything was fine at the chalet and she wasn't to hurry home on their account. She sent Jim a telegram: 'Meet me tomorrow evening train in town sleep there.'

Jim went. Kate jumped nimbly down from the train; they took hold of each other's hands, gazed at one another and laughed for joy. She said:

'Don't let's say anything serious just yet.'

She did, however, say that Jules had kept an eye on her quite adorably for Jim, while he was away.

They had taken adjacent rooms, because of police regulations. Kate made Jim sit beside her on the couch, and said:

'Well, here we are. You're my Jim, and I'm your Kate. Everything's all right now. But when I saw you at tea here, six weeks ago, you talked to me about your business matters; well, I've got mine, too. You told me you'd been saying good-bye to your girls; I've been saying good-bye to my lovers. You're going to hold me in your arms all night – but that's all. We want a child, don't we, Jim? Well, if you gave me one now – I wouldn't know for sure – that it was yours. You understand, Jim, don't you?'

She was watching him intently.

Jim understood; and was shattered. She was in the very middle of his heart, drinking and drinking . . . Let her drink! Jim, too sad to be angry, felt all his love ebbing out of him.

She went on:

'Jim, I had to. I did it for us. I had to put things straight between us. I suspected – no, I was certain, that you'd been consoling the girls you were leaving behind in Paris; consoling them *à la* Jim! I couldn't go on being engaged to you if I hadn't consoled (*à la*

Kate, we do it in the same way, Jim!) the man, or the men, that
*I* was leaving behind. I told Albert to go to my sister's house, and
I joined him there; and in myself, with him, I wiped out every
trace of your infidelity. So now everything's right between us,
Jim; we're quits.'

'Do you love Albert?' said Jim.

'No,' said Kate, 'though he's got lots of good points.'

'Does he love you?'

'Yes.'

Jim was weighing things up. Yes, he had made certain farewells,
just as Kate thought. Yes, he had done it without affecting his love
for Kate in any way. Perhaps Kate had done the same without
affecting her love for him? Jim accepted the equality Kate was
offering. He could feel that she loved him as he loved her, that there
wasn't any question of more or less, only that there was a single
force drawing them together. And, like Kate, he wiped out the past.

They were trembling with desire, but chaste. And chaste they
had to remain throughout this long night of love. And throughout the succeeding nights, until Kate knew for certain that she
had not conceived Albert's child.

'Admirable!' said Jules to Jim. 'Such tremendous manœuvres!
What excitements you invent for yourselves!'

Their self-imposed restraint raised them both into an exalted
mood. They regarded their abstinence as a vow, a question of
honour, of keeping faith with themselves. Each of them in turn,
when the other showed signs of weakening, saw to it that honour
was maintained intact. They stayed together all the time, there
was no cheating. The promised land was in sight.

The promised land abruptly receded.

All three of them had gone to town to see the lawyer who had arranged for the divorce, and who was going to look after the marriage as well. They regarded their journey as a pleasure-trip, and the legal details as a mere formality.

Shocked by the gaiety and perfect understanding of the three accomplices, the lawyer pushed his spectacles further up on his nose, stared at them and said:

'There is still some time to elapse before the decree becomes absolute. What's more, the future child would be legally attributed to the first husband if it was born before a certain date, the date in question depending on that of the divorce and being calculated in accordance with the maximum length of the period of gestation observed in women.'

'What?' said Kate, who had hardly been listening to this legal discourse.

The lawyer translated it into terms of dates. They must wait nearly two months before begetting the said child. The marriage itself would have to be later still, but at least the child would be legitimized by it.

The three were dumbfounded. Jules asked if there wasn't some legal provision which could be invoked against him, but was told there wasn't.

Kate and Jim didn't prolong their vow, but were ravaged by having to prevent the conception of the child. They were ashamed to be obeying the civil law instead of the law of their own natures.

Except for this big shadow across their path, life at the chalet resumed its normal course, with its games, its peace, its emotional abundance.

Kate read to them long passages of her diary of last year, from Jim's arrival to his departure for Paris. It was as intricate as a Hindu temple, a labyrinth in which it was easy to get lost.

Jim's diary was as clear as a table of contents by comparison. Jules and Jim treated Kate respectfully.

'If you both wrote the story of your relationship – but wrote it separately and fully, you from your own irreducible point of view, Kate, and you from yours, Jim, and published them together, it would make a very unusual book,' said Jules.

She gave them a performance of the dance-number which she had devised in her studio in town. They didn't think much of it.

'It needs the atmosphere of a crowded bar,' she said; 'all that smoke and excitement.' Perhaps – or perhaps she hadn't worked at it at all and had been seeing Albert instead. But Jim didn't like to think about that.

She and Jim inhabited successively all the beds and bedrooms in the chalet, even including Jules's little monastic cell; she requisitioned them one after the other. She finally opted for a wide peasant-style bed with pillars and a ceiling, decorated with gigantic flowers and fruit by a peasant artist.

Some drawings of Kate's were attracting attention in a little review which had recently been started. She was always with Jim, even when she was working; the slightest movement of her lips, even without raising her eyes from the drawing, brought Jim to her side to quench her thirst for love. They made themselves believe that their every caress was in some way a preparation for the child. This put a strain on them and they looked a little haggard.

There was a late fall of snow. They woke up one sunny morning to see the park covered in a thick eiderdown of white. Kate was the first to notice; she called everyone, stripped off her pyjamas on the steps outside and dived naked into the new snow. She disappeared in it, wallowed, turned somersaults, bit at the snow and ate it.

'When you're older,' she told the little girls, 'you'll be able to greet the snow like this with me.'

Jules and Jim were afraid that in rolling on the snow-covered lawn, where there were some short stakes in the ground, she would hurt herself – but, without seeming to pay attention, she evidently remembered perfectly where each of them was.

A telegram announced that Fortunio was coming for twenty-four hours. He arrived that evening. From the time he was seventeen, Jules and Jim had taken him for long romantic walks in Paris, the Paris of the poets, and they regarded him as a younger brother; he addressed them, however, as 'Father Jules' and 'Father Jim'. Six years later he had been Kate's lover, almost under Jules's eyes. But how could they blame him? Kate chose her lovers and took them, she wasn't taken by them, really – and by that time she had been able to tell Fortunio, truthfully, that there wasn't much left to be spoiled in her love for Jules.

Fortunio confronted them in a big, light green, checked over-coat, with his flowing, caressing voice, his lilies-and-roses complexion, and his slightly floppy air, like a young pedigree dog.

'Where shall we put him to sleep?' said Jules.

'With us,' said Kate.

Jules knew there wasn't a spare bed in the house; but Kate had said 'with us', and it was therefore no concern of his. He went up at his usual time to his bachelor bedroom, as he always got up early.

Kate, Jim and Fortunio went on talking till late at night in the four-poster. Kate said:

'We can all three sleep in this big bed.'

'Why not?' they said.

Jim could feel that Kate wanted to make an experiment. All right then! He'd make it too.

They turned out the light and lay down in the sudden darkness. The sheets had a fresh, pleasant smell. So had Kate. She had put herself in the middle. Fortunio had been lent a pair of pyjamas. Jim remembered Magda and the night of the ether.

They went on talking for a bit and then were silent. Kate's right hand was holding Jim; he was sure her left was holding Fortunio; comparisons . . . Should he put the light on again – the hanging switch was dangling and swinging just behind his head? No, that would have been poor style. They were free, all of them. They were playing pitch and toss with their lives, and he was ready to give Kate up without lifting a finger to resist. Fortunio was ready for anything Kate wanted. Jim thought to himself, 'If she lends herself to Fortunio, I'm set free.' The silence and Kate's imperceptible manœuvres dragged on, and Jim no longer wanted to have a child by her.

Kate turned her head in Fortunio's direction, said aloud, 'Good-night, Fortunio,' and kissed him. She turned towards Jim and was no doubt going to do the same with him, but he was already whispering in her ear:

'At the time when I still wanted a child from you—'

'What!' said Kate, 'what's this time you're talking about?'

'It was just ten minutes ago.'

Kate sprang astride Jim, almost fell out of the bed, pushed him into the middle and forced herself into his arms, lying to the right of him.

'Go on, Jim,' she said expectantly.

'There's nothing more to say.'

She twined herself round him. Jim respected Fortunio's presence and they went to sleep. They all felt fine when they woke up. Fortunio behaved charmingly and then left.

Kate was reading aloud to Jules and Jim the passage about the child drowned in the lake, from Goethe's *Kindred by Choice*. Her tears began flowing, and that made a tear run down Jim's cheek too. Anything associated with 'child' was too much for them. Jules pitied them.

Jim read them a poem, *Daphnis and Chloe*.

CHLOE

Is there then no more to know,
Daphnis,
Than lying in each other's arms
And sleeping so?

DAPHNIS

Yes, Chloe, there is more to know
And more to do:
There's taking you –
Which, till now, I never knew.

CHLOE

Is there then no more to do,
Daphnis, than what you never knew –
This taking me?

DAPHNIS

Yes, Chloe, there is more to do:
There's lying in each other's arms
And sleeping so.

Kate said, 'I like the way it goes round in a circle.'

Jules said, 'It's like a literal translation from several languages simultaneously.'

Jim said the frontiers between languages ought to be abolished. They made up some short poems in a mixture of three languages, just as things came into their heads, as in dreams. Jules and Jim invented a new continent of their own, Austrasia; but Kate's poems declared there must be more ruins and more wars.

'You're good Europeans,' Jules said to them. 'It's only right inside your love that you're nationalists.'

This nerve-racking period of waiting went on for a long time.

Life was no longer at 'set fair' for Kate and Jim, it was undependable and insecure. The calmest sky would suddenly reverberate with thunder, and Kate would be overwhelmed by destructive rage. She needed battles and bloodshed.

Her face would be ravaged instantaneously by doubt, and her expression became terrifying; the archaic smile turned into a knife-gash.

At such times Jules took care of her like an invalid. He regarded these crises as a sacred malady which was dangerous for her and for them all, an 'earthquake of the soul'. In Kate's family there had been both highly gifted people and apparently unmotivated suicides.

And whenever Jim was too happy she was under a compulsion to strike him down.

One day when she was feeling beatific, they went to town together. In order to get their tiresome errands done quicker and have time for fun afterwards, Jim suggested that he should go on his own to get a document which was needed in connection with the marriage, while she went shopping.

After all, she liked being left alone in town, with the reins loose on her neck; she enjoyed being treated as something that can't be stolen. She got into a taxi; as it was moving off she said to Jim, who was running along by the window – said it right into his face as he was coming close for a kiss:

'And now I'm going to do something really irreparable.'

They had arranged to meet for tea, but she didn't appear; he didn't see her till the evening, at the chalet.

She won them back to her by the joy she showed at being with Jim again. She said she hadn't done anything. Jim believed her. Jules didn't, precisely because she had completely got over her crisis and was fond and warm with Jim. 'What of it?' thought Jules, 'it's her way of loving.'

At the end of a meal Jules did something which was unusual for him; he made a mildly bawdy joke about a nightdress of Kate's. Jim disliked this; and Kate took it as a heinous insult, both to himself and to love. She was utterly contemptuous of both Jules and Jim, and it was no use for Jim to point out that he hadn't said anything; whenever she had anything to reproach one of them with she always included the other, as if they had been one person. Jules put on a contrite face but wanted to laugh.

'My charming little Boche,' Jim said to Kate, 'you're always declaring war on me.'

'With good reason!' she replied.

Lucie was staying in the city not far away where Jim had first got to know her. He hadn't seen her for seven years. The war had been a bad time for her. Her parents were dead and her family had lost all their money. She saw Jules first, alone; when he came back in the evening he reported that she was still the same Lucie but had altered a good deal. She was the same age as Jim, eight years older than Kate. She came to see them. Jules told her what had been going on.

Jim was upset to see that Lucie had aged. She had been working with those beautiful hands of hers. After lunch, all four went and sat out in the park. Kate devoted a moment to making it cruelly clear that these two men, who had loved her, were now hers, Kate's. But Lucie was no longer living on that plane, her strength came from elsewhere. She knew that even now, when they had been carried away by the whirlwind that was Kate, they still had inside them the sources of their former love for her, Lucie. She gave Kate credit for vitality and daring, but no more.

Kate told her about the divorce and her engagement to Jim. She had a theory to argue: certain women who felt they had a vocation for it were in duty bound, for the benefit of the race, to have a child by such and such a man, when they felt instinctively that he was the right one; but they couldn't bring up all their children themselves, they weren't necessarily gifted in that direction. She asked whether Lucie would be willing to bring up the child she was going to have with Jim. Lucie was silent for a moment, then she said:

'I'd do it if Jim asked me to, and provided the child was entrusted to me absolutely, once and for all.'

Jim admired Lucie for saying this.

Lucie was living alone nowadays in her big house; part of it was let off, and she had kept only the attics for herself. She invited them to come and see her if they were passing that way. Jim accepted, and Kate seemed to have no objection.

When Lucie had gone, Kate said, 'Tranquillity's a mask. Mask for mask, I prefer violence.'

Jules still felt a little bitter towards Lucie for having so persistently refused him. He was thinking of the straightforward, stable life he would have had with her, if she had been willing. Jim at present was living only for Kate and the children they would have. Perhaps Lucie was thinking, 'Jim and Kate won't stay together indefinitely.'

# 8

## *The Villa Edgar Allan Poe*

Kate took Jim away to the capital. She pointed out the house where she was born, and entertained him with childhood memories.

They ran into Fortunio, and together they visited bars where sailors were dancing with sailors, and others where typists were dancing with typists. There were also bars that stayed open all night in defiance of regulations; the possibility of a police raid, and all the lights going out suddenly, was regarded by regular customers as an extra attraction. They saw a clandestine and thoroughly modest ballet-performance by naked girls, which was a masterpiece; and the others of the same sort which were not. Jim, to his companions' surprise, rapidly wearied of this night-life and elected to spend his evenings 'at home'.

'Home' was a well-built, red-and-black-brick villa consisting of a single tall storey overlooking a large garden-cum-courtyard, in a middle-class residential district; Kate's elder sister Irene had lent it to her. It contained an enormous drawing-room with a verandah, a music-room and two big bedrooms. The furniture was a mixture, some opulent and some just comfortable. The cabinets and cupboards were stuffed with things which had been kept for old times' sake, notably some ten or eleven romantic hats which had adorned Irene. She was a widow, and lived with her five children in a handsome country house, an hour's journey away. The villa was their base whenever they came to town.

Looking through the family albums, Jim had seen a photo of Irene as a girl, and he had the impression that but for Kate, who was six years younger, he might have been attracted to her. Irene's smile, though not archaic, was captivating, and her glance was level. Since becoming a widow she had lived in a little circle of suitors and would-be lovers.

Kate took Jim for a few days to stay with her. He knew that Albert, only a few months previously, had spent two days there with Kate. The two sisters were born rivals, but nevertheless, on principle, helped each other in their love-affairs. Irene flirted with Jim, despite the presence of her court and her sister.

Irene's tall children were handsome. Kate and Jim spent a whole night with the two eldest on a lake, in their sailing-boat, and the young men wrapped them up to sleep in the spare sail. At dawn they played tennis with cardboard beer-mats at an inn on the lakeside.

Kate's nephews kissed her like lovers. The whole household spoke disapprovingly of Irene's wild ways, but everyone loved her.

The villa, which was odd enough in itself, became even more like something out of Edgar Allan Poe, in Jim's eyes, because of the following incidents.

With a cigar in his mouth, he was daydreaming on the verandah; in front of him was the long dark brick wall separating the garden-cum-courtyard from the courtyard of the house next door. It seemed to him as if the wall was no longer at right angles to the ground. He rubbed his eyes. With a surprisingly gradual movement the wall heeled over, turning on its own base, and crashed down throughout its length on to shrubs, hen-coops and bicycles, with a dull crunch. Dust went up in a cloud.

Next morning when Jim was lying asleep with Kate in his arms, he felt as if the dust from the wall was rising from the parquet flooring in the room, and as if he was swallowing Kate's hair which was tickling his throat. He opened his eyes and saw a lovely pink-ish mist rolling in whirls just over their heads. 'What a funny dream!' he thought. Then he understood it was real; the top of the room was full of dense smoke and the rising sun was tinting it through the window. It was only near the floor that the air was still clear. The smell of burning brought him wide awake. The weight of Kate's body was holding him prisoner; he shook her, gently.

'Kate! Something's burning.'

Kate opened one eye, sniffed the smoke, sized up the situation, and shut her eye again.

'Kate, if the heat breaks the windows the whole place'll go up.'

'Be quiet a moment, Jim. I can guess what it is.'

'Well, what?'

'It's that wretched untidy Irene. One day she stood her gas-cooker on a slatted wooden packing-case full of straw and cottonwool, and it's been standing like that for the last five years. Last night, when dinner was cooking, this wretched Kate, or this wretched Jim, must have dropped a match which hadn't had time to go out properly, through the slats, so there's a fire smouldering in the packing-case.'

'Oughtn't we to go and see?'

'Oh, not now we've settled down,' and Kate snuggled back to go to sleep again.

Jim couldn't help laughing.

They did go, however, because the smoke bothered them. They poured water on the packing-case, but that was no good; in the end they dragged it with some difficulty to the window and threw it out. During the whole operation Kate, stark naked, was much defter and more efficient than Jim.

Late one night, two slightly tipsy barons came to call on Kate. Jim didn't want to get up, so Kate received them on her own. Jim, from his bed, could hear their noisy laughter; they were making various suggestions to Kate, the mildest of which was that she should let them throw her Frenchman out of the window. Jim thought about putting in an appearance in the drawing-room to see what was going on, but he was too lazy to dress. Kate was entertained by this conversation and was keeping it going with drink. She was very sensitive to alcohol, and he didn't like to see her going in for a combination of liqueurs and barons.

When the visitors had left, he gently said as much. She took umbrage. They clashed, promptly and energetically as always, and inside two minutes a storm was in progress. Kate mentioned Gilberte and Jim replied, 'Gilberte equals Jules.' Kate riposted, 'Gilberte equals Albert.' The situation became ugly.

They heard Jules, who was there on a few days' visit, come back from the theatre and go to bed in the next room.

'You and Jules!' said Kate. 'What wonderful psychologists! You can write things down for them in black and white but it's a waste of time, they read them without understanding a word and give knowing little winks at each other.'

'For example?' said Jim.

Was it because she had had a drink? Kate resolved to strike right home.

'For example,' she said, 'in my diary of last year, the day before you went away, the afternoon when you went to that film by yourself, I wrote: "I went to Harold's flat, and there came a moment when he placed his hands on my body, one on each side" – ' (she repeated her words, pointing at the hands with her eyes and then raising her face to an imaginary Harold) – 'One . . . on each . . . side . . . of me – well, if that's not plain enough for you, what would be?'

She was kneeling on their big bed, with her head high and her hair down, gazing into Jim's eyes. He could read in hers that it was true.

So she had done this to him at the height of their love, at the height of his trust in her; and she had been saving up this poison in secret, in spite of their confessions and 'new starts'.

Something inside Jim was crashing into pieces, like the wall. At the same time he could feel his right hand getting heavy. With the palm flat he brought it hard against Kate's face, and she was thrown across the bed. His eye lighted on the twin dimples of her loins, the dimples he knew and loved so well, and he treated each of them to a direct hit – and found himself surprised, as ever, by how yielding yet springy Kate's flesh was.

She gave a yell.

There was a knock on the door.

Jules's voice, from the drawing-room, asked, 'What's the matter? Do you need me?'

'No! Thank you all the same, Jules,' called Kate, getting up bruised and radiant from the bed.

'At last!' she sighed to Jim, 'at last a man who dares to beat me when I deserve it! You do love me, Jim!' She buried her face in his chest.

He pushed her away, but not for long. Nevertheless the picture of Harold's hands remained obstinately in the back of his mind, and every time they had a row he wondered, 'How much more is she hiding from me?'

For several days Kate had a sore back; her face was swollen, and she went into town to flaunt it in the eyes of the world.

Jim had suffered a worse blow than any he had dealt. Ought he to apply the law of retaliation?

An opportunity presented itself at once. Kate had to stay a day and night at her sister's house in order to see their lawyer. Irene doubled neatly in her tracks and confronted Jim in the villa at noon, at the precise moment when Kate was arriving at the country house to find a note from her. Jim couldn't do less than invite Irene to lunch.

She was wearing a summer dress which showed off her full, healthy figure, and a romantic hat which was a worthy successor to the collection in the cupboard. She was in high spirits: to satisfy a whim she had bought a charming meadow and a wooded hill, at a fancy price for which her family had reproached her, and now the galloping devaluation of the mark had turned her purchase into a brilliant stroke of business.

Jim and Irene saw a street-barrow loaded with red roses. Jim presented her with a bunch without so much as thinking of their traditional meaning.

She had the charm and light-heartedness of a Creole or a spoilt child, contrasting strongly with the serious Kate. She announced her intention of sleeping in one of the villa's two bedrooms (it was her house, after all), and said there was a film she wanted to see. Jim offered to take her. She accepted at once, and it was further agreed that they should have a little supper afterwards in an amusing place she wanted to show him.

At tea she talked to him about Kate and their childhood and their different attitudes to life: how they admired each other but agreed about nothing – not even love.

At this point Jim, thinking of the coming night, considered it prudent to mention that in some cases he believed in fidelity and that he, at least, observed it where Kate was concerned. 'Bravo!' said Irene, with a challenging smile. Jim became aware that she was determined to have some fun, and that she was going to make a dead set at him. She was wearing a tropical perfume, and her nose and chin were a more feminine variant of Kate's.

And, now that he thought of it, what a marvellous revenge he could take on Kate by sleeping with Irene! What a dagger he could drive home where it hurt most, to make her realize what it felt like, and to cancel the memory of Harold's exploring hands!

During the minute following his declaration of fidelity, Jim abandoned himself in spirit to Irene. He would even have preferred matters to come to a head at once, without film or supper.

Their complicity was firmly established by the time they got back to the house.

Whom did they find sitting at the piano, pale-faced, in red silk pyjamas, playing a sonata by Beethoven with the serious application of a child? Kate in person.

As soon as she had found Irene's letter, Kate, knowing her sister and her Jim, had set off without lawyer or lunch, had taken the only train which would get her back to town that day, and was waiting for them.

Kate was severe to Irene, who was meek. In their sisterly quarrels it was always Kate who won. Irene retired to her room and telephoned another lover.

To Jim, Kate was extraordinarily indulgent; she understood, she forgave him – all the more readily in that he'd done nothing! Like a young mother who, in a shop, tells her little boy that he can't have the cake he wants, and gives him a nicer one made at home (he mustn't cry, he's got to realize that this one is better for him), she devoted herself to Jim, and watching him carefully made him free of all her charms, till little by little she had divested him of the last shred of his desire for Irene.

So peace was made between them without Jim having carried out his retaliation.

# 9

## *Walking in Darkness*

They went back to the chalet. Spring was over, summer had come again. The divorce proceedings were through; Kate and Jim would soon be able to start a child which wouldn't bear Jules's surname. At that period marriages between nationals of Jim's and Kate's respective countries still entailed a mass of difficult formalities. 'What of it?' thought Jim. 'Let's beget the child; we'll have time to comply with the marriage-regulations before it's born.'

They went out for a walk with the little girls. Near the village a gipsy was exhibiting a couple of monkeys in a little enclosure and the girls went in to give them nuts. The bigger of the monkeys jumped on to Lisbeth's shoulders, took the nuts from her and pulled her hair. Jim was throwing a leg over the barbed wire, about to intervene, but Kate had already slipped underneath and was driving the monkey away. 'How quick she is!' he thought.

That evening, at table, the conversation turned on animals which live in caves or at the bottom of the sea. Kate told her daughters:

'There are no monsters, because they don't know they're monsters in the eyes of the others. They're as innocent as we are, they love their little ones as we do; God made them like that. He's the loving Father of snakes, and thieves, and murderers.'

And they were all filled with compassion for monsters.

In a sports shop where they had been buying a few things, Kate, with a sudden, resolute gesture, stole a little compass and showed it proudly to the children afterwards.

'That's the beginning of a slippery slope,' said Jim.

'It's such fun,' she said, 'and besides, we paid for everything else!'

At last the date came when the child could legally be conceived. They were almost taken by surprise by the freedom they had been waiting for so expectantly. They had gone into training for it, choosing their food carefully, leading a healthy life and excluding any other objective from their minds. They had practically decided when the birth was to take place. They created their child reverently. They felt free, like a pair of wild animals, in the park at night – and in their den, the four-poster with its primitive paintings.

In due course they were astonished to find that Kate wasn't pregnant. Jules made fun of them, affectionately.

'It's like golf,' said Kate, 'if you're over-confident you spoil your shot.'

In a more chastened frame of mind they started again. They were Adam and Eve, at the beck and call of their instincts.

A month later, they knew once again that 'the Lord had not blessed their union'.

This time it was a shock.

They went to be examined by a specialist, who told them they were quite normal and that there was no reason why they shouldn't have children. The word 'normal' was almost offensive to them. In this realm, they didn't like thinking of themselves as average. The doctor told them that they must learn to wait, that there were imponderable factors in all such situations, and that many couples proved fertile only after several months.

*

Kate and Jim did their best to be patient. They began working again; Kate drew and Jim wrote. After work they went deep into the woods and made love, and Jim picked Kate up by the feet and shook her gently, as one might shake down a sack of nuts, to increase their chance of having a baby. They felt they were at one with the brotherhood of grass, stones, trees and stars.

The next moon brought them a further disappointment.

Jules told them, 'Well, you may have children. But perhaps it just isn't one of your talents.'

Kate concluded that the chalet was an unfavourable environment.

In the first days of October they went off to an historic town; their journey was a spiritual pilgrimage, attended by nature at her most limpid.

Doubts as to their vocation as parents were beginning to gnaw at them. Even Jules had begotten his first child sooner. They went on, of necessity, with the legal formalities of their marriage, but Kate had forgotten to bring her papers with her; Jim took this as a pointer.

Judging from old photos of Kate during pregnancy, and from Jules's description, Jim thought Kate was never so much herself as when she was expecting a baby. Jim had an inward need to be devoted to a different Kate from the one he was with; a Kate round, fertile and appeased. An empty space was developing between them, a void which their embraces could no longer fill for more than a moment.

Of course they amused themselves as before. They shot at crows (but never hit them) with a revolver, and with slings. They held each other in their arms. But they were waiting for the next disappointment. What would they do when it came?

'What's the use of getting married unless one has children?'

was the ground-swell of Jim's thoughts. 'We used to think of them, all handsome and healthy, a whole houseful of them; them, and Jules, and the little girls and Mathilde; and spare rooms for any friends who liked to come and see us . . . Perhaps Kate will go back to her escapades if we don't have children.'

Would they start working again in earnest? It was only for their children's sake that they wanted success.

Kate, for her part, was thinking thoughts which she kept to herself. Sometimes she went to have coffee, alone, at a bar. She took Jim there and introduced a boxing instructor to him, a short, energetic man, agile and cunning.

They went to his gymnasium and watched some good bouts. Jim boxed with him, hit him once, was hit several times himself, and was finally overwhelmed and willingly admitted the other man's superior speed and skill.

In between times, the boxer taught Kate the difficult art of cheating at cards. She showed promise; Jim showed none, and he could feel in the bar an atmosphere in which Kate moved easily and he did not.

After dinner one evening, Jim unluckily let Kate go up to their bedroom alone while he stayed in the dining-room; he was reading a financial paper and wanted to finish it. He and Kate, with their tiny resources, had risked a miniature speculation, and it seemed to be turning out well. The question was whether to sell out at once or not. He joined Kate, expecting to find her in bed. She was dressed, made-up and ready to go out; her eyes were hard and smiling at once. She asked Jim if he wanted to go with her, but this was for form's sake only; he had 'flu. She said she would be back in half an hour.

After an hour Jim had finished doing his sums. He had a foreboding: Kate had slipped out of his grasp like an eel. After two hours he was very anxious. By the time another hour had gone by he was convinced that she had gone to *do something really irreparable*, as her saying was. And now Jim set about the pyramid of their love and, stone by stone, began demolishing it. His account of this night, written shortly afterwards in his notebook, filled several pages. He had a temperature and his ears were singing. In this condition he couldn't go running after Kate, and in any case he didn't want to. Kate never admitted that illness existed, and now it was his turn to be ill.

Kate gave him plenty of time to think; it was two in the morning when, all smiles, she came back to their room. She had 'had a tremendous game of cards with the boxer and his friends'. Jim thought of hitting her, but had neither the strength nor the will-power. He just wanted to get away.

He told Kate he was afraid the boxer might lead her astray.

'I told the boxer about our unhappiness.' (Jim shuddered.) 'He suggested giving me a child himself, without your knowing.' (Jim heard this with horror.) 'But I'm waiting for one from you.' As she said these words she raised her eyes to his, and he believed her.

It was near the end of November. The legal arrangements had broken down; there was always some fresh detail required for the records. Did they really still want to get married? Snow was falling, and the hotel was badly heated. They both wanted a home, but not the same home. They were once more waiting to know whether a child had been granted to them. If only it had, how quickly everything would have been all right!

Two days later, it was certain once again that Kate was not pregnant.

Jules was writing letters to her, asking her to come and stay with him and his mother, in the capital. Jim had no idea what she might have written to Jules. Jim was ill, and longing to be looked after by his own mother, in the bed he had slept in when he was a student.

They decided, without committing themselves about the future, that each of them would go home.

At the last moment, when her luggage was already in the cloak-room, Kate postponed her departure for a day and took Jim for a long walk in the countryside, with melting snow underfoot. The walk was as unforgettable as the one which was the prelude to their love.

But, during this one, Kate talked of nothing but Jim, deliber-ately bringing out all the grudges which she had been piling up against him. The Jim she portrayed to him was selfish, stingy, too cautious. There was a certain amount of truth in it, Jim thought; and also a certain amount of unfounded *lèse-majesté*. Her accus-ation as a whole was a model of both clarity and composition. When she came to their last month together, here in this little town, Kate could restrain herself no longer; her indignation burst out, especially with regard to his feebleness in the legal prepar-ations for marriage – which surprised Jim, since in his opinion his documents were nearer to completion than Kate's.

Kate wound up by saying that he had made a fool of her, and that the only thing she wanted now was to get back to the tender, generous protection of Jules.

Jim could have said a lot in reply, but he preferred to think things over. Besides, as he hadn't given her a child, he was in the wrong.

They spent this last night together in a tiny hotel at the station, in a narrow, hard bed. They didn't speak. They took each other once more, without knowing why; perhaps just to put a full-stop at the end of the chapter. It was as if they were burying some-thing, or as if they were already dead themselves.

For the first time, Jim was faced with an immobile, frigid Kate, and he gave himself to her unwillingly.

\*

Jim took Kate to her train. This time they didn't wave their hand-kerchiefs.

Jim was glad she was going to Jules. If only their failure could bring her back to Jules for good!

Kate was going. He hadn't managed to keep her. He didn't even want to any more. Was it all finished now?

He was alone. He felt as if a huge stone had been lifted off his chest. He breathed deeply. At the base of one lung he felt a sudden stab of pain.

Kate would have liked him to have not only his own qualities but those of Jules as well – and others besides. What he would have liked her to have was the certainty and steadiness of Lucie.

They weren't reasonable people.

# PART 3

## *To the Very End*

I

# Separation?

By the time Jim got to his mother's house in Paris he was really ill. He got into the bed he had slept in as a student, and stayed there for three weeks with aching bones and a high temperature. The painful place in his lung started to get better. He got up and went out; and relapsed for a month.

His doctor questioned him intelligently about his recent life; it was a year since they had seen each other. Jim gave an outline. Apart from the last few weeks he had never been so well. The doctor said:

'You've thoroughly overstrained yourself; you've been living every side of your life in a state of excessive euphoria, and now your tissues have gone on strike and are forcing you to take a complete rest. At present you're at the mercy of any little draught or the slightest emotional upset.'

Contemplated from his sick-bed, the last eight months seemed to Jim to have been crammed with delight, but also with exhausting exertions. The present truce with Kate was a necessity.

He had written asking news of them both. She replied with a short letter, praising Jules's tender ways. One sentence seemed to leave the door open on vague possibilities. Jules, on his side, answered reticently; he didn't want to influence them in any way. He didn't know whether Kate and Jim were just having another quarrel or were in process of breaking up. Jim wondered whether Kate and Jules had started living together again. For Jules's sake he hoped they had. Was Kate seeing anything of Albert, or Harold, or some other man? He thought she probably was. In his present state he felt any barrier between himself and Kate was a protection.

It was winter.

An incredible note arrived from Kate: 'I think I'm pregnant. Come.'

'But who by?' wondered Jim.

He was in bed because of his relapse, and incapable of getting up. He wrote and told Kate. He was in any case no longer keen on going to see her, pregnant as she was by some other man, most likely, for their pitiful farewell night could scarcely have succeeded where the full blaze of their love had failed.

Jules wrote very briefly, saying that Kate wanted to see him and didn't believe in his illness. This irritated Jim: she judged other people by herself. He wrote to her, expressing his doubts about the child's paternity (if indeed she really had started a baby), basing his doubts on their past, and the boxer, and Kate's first letter after their parting.

Fate was at their doors, knocking, knocking.

They had a dialogue of the deaf. Their letters took three days on the way. Jim had hardly posted his packet of doubts when he got a radiant letter from Kate, the utterance of a young woman who was fruitful at last and gave heartfelt thanks to God; she convinced him that for the sake of herself and her spiritual security and her life with the child which was now growing in her womb, she had given herself to Jim and to Jim alone. Still more than by her actual words, Jim was overcome by the innocent, defenceless attitude underlying them. To him she was like a lamb. He wrote to her and planned to go to her as soon as he could stand on his feet.

Meanwhile Kate received his harsh, doubting letter and thought it was his reply to her own gentle one. She was devastated, became angry again and stung him like a wasp in a letter announcing a final break between them.

Hardly had she posted it when she received Jim's sweet-natured letter, expressing his belief in her and saying that he was coming. She believed for the first time that his illness was real, and was sorry for him.

But Jim had had her violent letter breaking up their relationship, and he replied confirming the break.

'Hard to starboard!' 'Hard to port!' They were steering their boats with great sweeps of the helm this way and that; eventually their pens dropped from their hands, like useless megaphones no longer audible above the storm.

They had vowed once that they would never telephone one another again, each dreading the effect of hearing the other's voice without the possibility of physical contact.

*He that killeth with the sword must be killed with the sword.* They had dealt each other mighty sword-thrusts in the past and they were doing it again now.

But he who has given loving smiles shall be saved by loving smiles. And they had given each other loving smiles in the past and they were doing it still.

For once Jim, who lingered in bed the whole of that winter, had no temperature and was sitting propped up against his pillows, thinking of Kate as a future mamma. She had once intimated for fun, in a shop, the way she would walk when pregnancy had swollen her body. Another time, she had sketched on a canvas the head of a tiny baby with straggling blond curls. He imagined Kate holding their child in her arms, and tears rose to his eyes. He didn't pay proper attention to what his visitors said to him, and answered distractedly; they went, worrying about him, and left him alone with his vision of his wife and their child.

In a black moment Kate wrote, 'Come at once. Perhaps the child will still be here.' Was this 'perhaps' a threat? It drained his small stock of energy. He couldn't set out on the strength of a 'perhaps'.

All their personal forces were under an eclipse.

A possibility arose of Kate coming to join him in Paris, but his mother, who knew about their life, made no secret of the fact that she thought it wrong. He was afraid of what might happen if they met. Kate would be wounded to the quick. Jim wrote to suggest that she stay in a near-by hotel to begin with, but she received this idea with suspicion.

There was a risk of their journeys crossing.

Jules was offering to re-marry Kate and bring up the child.

'Ah,' Jim thought sometimes, 'it's a fine thing to rediscover the laws of human life; but how practical it must be to conform to the existing rules!'

The child, wearied by this alternation of heaven and hell before it had even had time to be born, perished a third of the way through its pre-natal life.

This news came to Jim in a note from Jules. Kate, from now on, wanted no communication with Jim.

So, in the end, they had created nothing.

Jim couldn't help being curious about Kate's unexpected pregnancy; he questioned his doctor, who said:

'It's possible for an ardent, well-suited couple not to have a child for a long time – and then to start one suddenly if for any reason, just a quarrel, for example, the woman happens to be frigid when they make love.'

Their last night together! The doctor's words were like a beam of light. For the first time, Jim really believed Kate.

He thought, 'We've been playing with the sources of life; turning them into weapons. So life has made us barren and left us rolling in the trough of the wave.'

He'd get the details one day if Jules was willing to tell him.

He convinced himself gradually that misfortune could have been averted if Kate and he had belonged to the same race and the same religion.

Fundamentally, they only communicated in translation. Words hadn't quite got the same meanings for them; nor even had gestures. At the worst moments, when their love was cracking under the strain, they no longer had any common ground. Their ideas of order, authority, and the roles of the sexes, were different.

They'd been daring, they'd tried to *bridge the gap*, their intentions had been good – but they'd hung on to their pride, they hadn't been apostles . . . Perhaps their son would have been one?

Kate and Jules weren't of the same race, either. Kate was purely Germanic; a fighting-cock who happened to have been born female. Jules was a Jew, one of those who, apart from a few close friends, avoid other Jews.

Six months passed. Jim had got back his strength. He started work again – in Paris, in his own city.

In June, Jules wrote to say that he and Kate had re-married.

So their home wasn't falling apart, Kate was with Jules, Albert had receded! Jim sent them his congratulations.

In August, he had occasion to visit their capital, where they were now living.

He wrote to ask Jules if he could see him. Jules answered 'Yes' – but that Kate preferred not to meet him.

Jim thought this quite natural.

## 2

## *White Pyjamas – In the Hamlet Country*

He was reunited with Jules in Jules's own city. Their old, uncomplicated relationship started up again instantly. It would have been beyond Jim's powers to say what Jules meant to him. In the past they had been nicknamed Don Quixote and Sancho Panza. When he was alone with Jules (just as it used to be when he had been alone with Kate), time disappeared for Jim. The most trifling things became completely satisfying. He enjoyed Jules's good cigar much more than his own. From the day they met, Jules had been teaching Jim something every moment of the time, without realizing it. He energized all Jim's sensibilities.

Jules was writing poems on the great Hindu deities.

Little by little, he talked about Kate. He had been afraid she was going to kill herself; she had bought a revolver and used to say, 'So-and-so died of suicide,' just as she might have said, 'He died of cholera.' Suicide, to her, was an invincible figure who rose up in front of you, like a praying mantis, and carried you off.

She knew that Jim had come and that Jules was seeing him, and she allowed Jules only a certain amount of time for the purpose; his daily round at home mustn't be interrupted.

One day, Jules gave Jim an invitation from Kate to come and have tea with them.

On his way, Jim asked himself whether he had left Paris on purpose to see her. He told himself he hadn't.

He found Kate withdrawn; something like a widow. Sometimes she gave a 'dead woman's smile', as she herself had said one day. She seemed more mature than of old; convalescent, more leisurely in her movements.

After tea she led Jim into Jules's big study and said to him:

'This winter I came in here alone and imagined you sitting at this desk. I aimed carefully, and fired. The bullet hit the wood, here, and the wall, there.' She showed him the two marks. Jules had told him nothing about this.

She made a weary gesture, and asked them both to come with her on an excursion the next day, to a lake not far away.

She told her maid, 'Do up my white silk pyjamas in a parcel.' And Jules carried this neatly tied parcel on his finger all day. Jim wondered what purpose it was to serve, and then forgot about it.

They walked in silence along avenues of fine trees. It was like walking behind a coffin. Jim could feel that Kate had an objective in mind. She and Jules appeared to be on good terms. She had re-married him. She was calm. At the moment when Jules booked the tickets, Kate raised her eyes fully to Jim's, for the first time. 'How much you destroyed!' she said. Jim was about to say something, but checked himself; his words would count for nothing.

They boarded a miniature train and reached the lake, among wooded hills, and followed its shore along paths intersected by tree-roots. On they walked, in the radiant late afternoon, and the links which had held their trio together trailed behind them, broken.

It seemed to Jim that behind her deep reserve Kate wanted to kindle a hope in him; but what could that hope be? They had had everything out between them on the eve of their separation, eight months ago, and what they'd said then was still valid for Jim, even more than their subsequent letters. What did she want? and why had he come?

Jules and Jim walked warily in the presence of Kate's melancholy. Like Ulysses tying himself to the mast to resist the song of the sirens, Jim had to brace himself to withstand the charm of Kate's voice.

In the dusk, at the water's edge, a restaurant suddenly lit up all its little lamps.

'I'm hungry. Suppose we have dinner here?' said Kate carelessly. She went along the line of little arbours and entered the last, which looked out on to the lake.

There, in a flexible rattan armchair, smoking, sat Harold.

'Neat!' thought Jim, stupefied.

'Good Lord, Harold,' said Kate, 'what are you doing here?'

'Enjoying the coolness,' said Harold, kissing Kate's hand and rapidly shaking those of Jules and Jim.

'Are you dining with us?' said Kate.

'With pleasure,' he said, 'provided it's at once.'

'You're meeting someone in town tonight?'

'Maybe.'

They sat down at the round table, Kate opposite Jules, between Harold and Jim.

Jim wondered whether Kate, manufacturing her own kind of justice, had devised a trick for getting him thrown into the lake. If she had, he'd defend himself.

The conversation between the three others was brilliant and quick and carried on in their own language. Jim missed a word here and there and gave up trying to follow.

Harold was very much the man of the world. He had had Kate as a girl, and again just before her marriage to Jules; he had also had her just before Jim went away for the first time, while Jim was at the cinema. Harold was the executor of Kate's revenges. Jim would have liked to box with him, to get to know him better. He tried to picture the bout.

Harold and Kate drank liqueurs.

After dinner they all went walking in the woods, at a lively pace. Kate leant for a moment on Jim's arm, getting a stone out of her shoe. What was she after?

Back to the station, into the little train, then town. They skirted a park, stopped in front of Harold's house and said good night. Kate shook Harold's hand, rejoined Jules and Jim; they turned to go. What on earth was the meaning of all this?

Kate suddenly remembered:

'Give me the parcel,' she said to Jules. He held it out to her, but the string had wound itself tight round his little finger; she undid it, snatched the parcel, went back to Harold, took his arm sweetly, wished a courteous 'Good night!' to Jim and Jules and accompanied Harold into the big porch, which engulfed them. The heavy door banged shut, and Jules and Jim were left gaping.

'Neatly played again!' said Jim; 'second tableau, including the white pyjamas this time. It took me by surprise.'

Kate had struck at them both together. Jim took Jules's arm and they walked on together.

'Ouf!' said Jim.

'Ouf!' Jules echoed gently.

'I suppose she had to,' said Jim. 'Still, I'm surprised she didn't choose a new man for the part, she's used Harold so many times already.'

'But why?' said Jules. 'Harold was just right for tonight.'

They went into a brasserie, drank cool beer, lit up long cigars, and pursued their bachelor conversation far into the night, without bringing Kate into it.

★

At noon the next day Jim was still in bed in his pretty little hotel room. He had been making plans for the next few months and writing letters in his head.

The porter came to tell him he was wanted on the telephone. Probably Jules. He ran to the booth at the end of the corridor.

'Jim! Jim! Jim!' It was Kate's voice, her warm voice of days gone by, her lioness-growl.

'Jim – what an awful night! Amusing, because of the circumstances, but it just showed me I was wasting my time. That kind of life, that state of mind – it's died on me. It was just a desert, Jim, there was nothing in it anywhere. I kept talking about you, Jim, I was trying to find you in it all, Jim. Is that really you? Are you listening to me?'

'Yes.'

'Then come. Now.'

Kate hung up.

Jim hesitated.

She was waiting for him in her drawing-room, radiant. Her having made fools of them the night before meant nothing at all, she was sure of herself again now, sure of life, she loved him as much as ever. The night had been a revelation. Her love for Jim had risen like a star, making everything pure. She told him about the night in detail, even putting in things which might have repelled Jim, using all her genius for telling a story.

As Jim listened he was thinking of the way they had suffered, last winter. Since then, he had heaped a good many spadefuls of earth on this love of theirs. She said, in passing:

'Children? We shall have as many as we want now. We've got a lifetime ahead of us.'

This broke the last dykes of Jim's resistance. She wasn't asking him what he thought, she was bearing him away with her. Like a naphtha-lake catching alight instantaneously, they were on fire for one another.

'What about Jules?' asked Jim at length.

'He loves us both. It'll be no surprise to him, and besides he'll suffer less this way. In the winter he was as unhappy as we were. We shall go on loving and respecting him . . . in our own way.'

There was a knock at the door. Jules's voice was saying:

'The children are waiting for you to have lunch.'

Jules came in. They were holding hands.

'Look at us, Jules,' said Kate, to make him a party to the situation.

Jules's eyebrows rose, a trifle sternly; but he showed no astonishment.

'Jules, Jim's lunching with us,' said Kate.

'All right, but come at once,' said Jules.

The little girls and Mathilde, infected by Kate's mood, hilariously made Jim welcome.

They spared Jules's home, but Kate often came to Jim, with Jules's knowledge, and stayed till midnight. And then it was hard for them to part.

Jules told Kate, 'I don't like being called a saint. A saint is someone you can load up like a donkey. No, I am not a saint! But what else can I do?'

Kate and Jim could no longer endure their self-imposed restraint. It was September. Kate said to Jim, 'We're off.'

'Where to?'

'Hamlet's country.'

They jumped into the next express. Standing in the corridor, they adored the flat landscape they were travelling through. They smoked, which was against the regulations printed on a little

enamelled notice. The ticket-inspector came along and levied a
fine, for which he gave them a receipt from a perforated pad.
Inflation was raging and the fine had gone down to almost nothing. They went on smoking; so did several other passengers
standing in the corridor. From time to time the inspector came
by and levied the fine again; the business had turned into a game
for the smokers. The inspector said, with a tranquil smile:

'From Monday next, there's going to be a different fine and I
shall be given a different pad.'

Jim admired the man.

They reached the Danish frontier and got out at a small resort,
scattered among the dunes. It was near the end of the season,
and the weather was fine. In spite of rationing restrictions the
hotel served them stews which were too big to get through.

The North Sea went out a long way and left a desert of sandy
ravines like gigantic cerebral convolutions, with deep channels
between the rounded plateaus. As the tide came in the channels
filled up with swirling currents and the water could cut off your
retreat. Kate loved getting encircled, it was fun; besides, Jim was
a poor swimmer, and she liked helping him along at her side.

She used to dive naked into the chill water, even after a big
meal. 'I've never had cramp yet,' she assured Jim.

One morning they found a narrow bank of smooth hard sand,
several miles long, with a little wooden structure visible at one
end of it. They were curious to know what it was, and walking
out there, found a fisherman's hut, empty, perched on long piles,
and fitted up with lights and reflectors. In front of it a seabird no
bigger than the palm of a hand, and as brilliant as a humming-
bird, was lying on its back, dead. It must have dashed itself against
one of the reflectors. 'Let's hope it's not an omen!' said Jim to
himself.

They got back just before the tide.

They never met anyone on the sandbanks, and Jim took photos
of Kate lying out there in the open, naked. He thought one of
them was the most beautiful he had ever seen. They were tempor-
arily short of money, and considered sending it in for a Kodak
competition. But though it was taken from behind it might have
been recognized as Kate, in the advertising displays in shop-
windows; so they refrained.

Ten days passed, between the blue of the sky and the yellow
of the sand. In such an atmosphere, the sting was taken out of
any little incidents which might formerly have led to misunderstandings.

On their journey back in the crowded train, Kate carelessly let
Jim's seat beside her own get taken by someone else, and Jim had
to spend several hours away from her, standing in the corridor.
Was she put out because he didn't make a fuss? Jim was surprised
at her having let another man take his seat; he thought for a
minute that it must be a war-pensioner. After that it was too late
to say anything.


They rejoined the family in their roomy quarters. Jim was officially shown round by Kate, the girls and Mathilde. The house
was sunny, looking out on to a wood and a spacious clearing. It
was Kate who had snapped it up the instant it came onto the
market. They told Jim the sequence of events.

When they first moved in, the large corner room had been
Kate's and Jules's bedroom, and the square room next to it had
been Jules's study. After these came a drawing-room and the
dining-room; the rest of the bedrooms were at the front of the
house.

Kate had done more and more entertaining, and Jules found
it got in the way of his work. He retreated, moving his study
from room to room in descending order of size. Then they started
having separate bedrooms. Jules, in love with solitude and harried

by Kate's activities, chose the only bedroom looking out on to the yard and said he'd use it as a study as well. He had shelves built all the way round it, from floor to ceiling, and moved all his books into them. In there he was a monk, very much at peace provided Kate didn't call him. He liked her to come and see him in his room, but not to bring people for him to meet. They had sub-let the place during the past two years, while they lived at the chalet, and had only taken it over again the previous autumn.

Jules had more of a share in Kate's life now that Jim was part of it too.

Jim made lengthy visits to Jules in his secluded room, listening to passages from his new books and helping him with his translations. Kate didn't object to their working together.

She, in the meantime, was painting on large white curtains, in a symbolic and more or less cubist style, the whole story of herself and Jim. Apart from a few realistic details an uninformed eye would have understood nothing. But after Kate, equipped with a long stick, had explained this pious itinerary to Jim, he could reconstruct any part of it at will and admire it at leisure.

Kate and Jules had taken Jim under their roof again, he no longer had to live in a hotel.

Two of Kate's women-friends were still in the country, and she wanted Jim to meet them. She often talked about them – exaggerating, according to Jules.

They were very different: one of them won prizes at horse-shows, the other was a social worker. Both were unmarried.

Kate liked picturing Jim in love with one or the other, imagining what he would say to them and they to him. This make-believe became a game which they played round the table at meal-times with Jules and the children. Little by little it acquired a certain reality in Kate's mind; she generously married Jim off, turn and turn about, with one or other of her friends. Jim laughed; he belonged to Kate.

Kate, with Jim, climbed the stairs to the Amazon's flat. With thumping heart, she paused on the landing before ringing the bell, and said:

'In ten seconds you'll be in love with another woman.' And she kissed him.

The Amazon had breeding, and lived her life with a dash. She gave them cocktails and conversation. She cared about almost nothing but horses. They accompanied her to an open-air *manège* at a barracks, where she rode a highly strung mare over timber fences whose height was put up after each jump. It was a fine sight, but it left Jim cold; and she for her part had no interest in a man who didn't ride. So nothing happened.

'In that case it'll be Angelica,' declared Kate.

As soon as they had come back from seeing the Amazon, she took Jim to see the nurse. Her rooms were bright and spotless. She was a girl with a mind and feelings of her own, devoted to her work; Jim, despite Kate's efforts to advertise him, made not the slightest impression.

'She's very reserved, things may develop yet; it's a matter of time,' said Kate after their visit. 'What about it, Jim? What do you think of her?'

'In her own way she's perfect,' said Jim. 'If she and I were cast up on a desert island we might eventually notice one another and start raising a family.'

Kate was at once relieved and disappointed. Jules followed the whole of this affair with more gravity than Jim; he brought his Hindu gods into it.

Jules often seemed to be fairly happy. They felt he was like a Buddha who knew them better than they did themselves. Sometimes, like

Laetitia, Napoleon's mother, he said, *'Pourvu que ça dure'* – 'May it last!'

Jules was much better than Jim at playing games of the make-believe kind with Kate. With the children they sang and acted German and French folksongs. It plucked at Jim's heart when they sang a French song, *The Sailor Came Home from the Sea* ('. . . *all unseen came he!'*), and the Fair Hostess bowed her head as the Sailor said to her:

> Three little ones he's given you: one more
> Is on the way, and that makes four!

Kate invented a game called 'The Village Idiot'. Everyone at table was the village, except Jim, who was the Idiot. The game consisted of talking to the Idiot and being frightened of him without letting him realise it, and also without upsetting him; at the same time it had to be made quite clear to everyone else just how idiotic he was. Kate in particular got everyone in fits of laughter. Jim was always slow to start laughing; he really did feel like the village idiot.

Kate came into the dining-room with Lisbeth and Martine. She was whistling, with a shrill note like a fife's, a rousing military march composed by Frederick the Great.

They marched round the table, like a miniature regiment. Kate told them wonderful stories about Frederick.

On her desk she had a heart-rending copy of the death-mask of that great unfulfilled idealist. The bony structure of his face was like her own.

She used to ask his advice before resolving on one of her punitive expeditions.

She would have liked him and Napoleon to have fought a battle against one another, for the sheer beauty of the duel.

# 3

## Retaliations – Venice

Jim made long visits to Paris, and this Kate accepted. He was publishing articles on the state of the contemporary theatre, a project which brought him frequently to Central Europe. He spent fortnights with Kate and Jules which kept him enchanted for months.

A year went by, a happy and almost uneventful year. Kate and Jim were now getting the benefit of their past battles; they had learnt to avoid such excesses. They abandoned themselves more easily to the great force propelling them. They were chaste after their own fashion and accepted life submissively. They distrusted the intellect. They clung to the example of Jules – quiet and industrious as a Benedictine monk.

They thought they were safe from themselves. But all the same, like the crack of doom, disaster fell.

One day they were visited from Paris by the son of a woman who had formerly played an important part in Jim's life, and who knew about their love. Out of consideration for Jules, as their host and Kate's husband, Jim hid his intimacy with Kate. She instantly inferred, 'If Jim's trying to hide our love from that woman's son, she must still be his mistress in Paris, whatever tale he may spin to me.'

White-faced, she rose, glanced at Jim with the smile indicating *something irreparable*, and went out.

'Poor Kate!' said Jules.

Jim had felt their inferno rising up again. He wanted none of it, he had had enough. He lay down on his bed with eyes shut and arms folded, thinking of how united they had been till a few moments ago. An hour passed.

He didn't see Kate come in and look at him, nor did he hear her feet on the carpet.

'That's enough, Jim,' she said gently. 'I thought you were deceiving me. So I've deceived you. It's over now.'

'What's over?'

'Our unhappiness. And your distress which makes me feel better.'

'What have you been doing?'

She told him. It was a man he didn't know, a painter who had tried to make love to her in the past and whom she had on a string. He had done her this service now, in a limited way without any possibility of consequences, but it was sufficient to make a compensation and restore the balance.

'But why?' said Jim. 'There was nothing to be compensated for.'

'To compensate for what I believed,' said Kate. 'And now I don't believe it any longer. But if I hadn't done anything I should always have believed it.'

'And what about my side of the balance?' Jim groaned.

'Jim! Tears!'

And Kate, radiantly happy, drank from his eyes; he hadn't realized till then that his eyes were wet. He saw her as an irresponsible animal, lapping up her natural drink. Ecstatically, she lived and moved and had her being in the red depths of his heart. He was without hope, he was drained dry.

Kate clasped him to herself all night, like a sick child. He went to sleep in her arms.

It was not until the next day that they were on their usual terms again.

\*

This new wound left Jim with bitter memories. During the following month he was in Paris. They wrote to each other as they would have talked.

Then there came a silence on Kate's side, followed by a letter from Jules which somehow conveyed embarrassment. Finally there was one from Kate, speaking of a balcony which could be climbed, and a terrace with flowers, all this wrapped round something else about which she told him nothing. This letter, on careful consideration, seemed to Jim to be as conclusive as the famous page in Kate's diary, in which she had mentioned Harold's hands; she was both telling and not telling (how good she was at that!), so as to be able to declare, 'I told you everything but you didn't understand.'

Jim decided to take action immediately, *à la* Kate. He sought out an actress with whom he had flirted ten years before (just as Kate would have done); a pretty woman, not tied down by convention. They didn't fall in love in the least; both of them were merely gratifying a whim and satisfying their curiosity. He savoured his revenge slowly, sip by sip. How nice and easy it all was! He spent a whole night with *the other woman*. Neither of them made any secret of being in love with someone else. Jim decided that what Kate said was true: it didn't matter whether you were very unfaithful or only a little, provided you did it *against your love*.

He tried to imagine the hours Kate had spent with Albert, and Harold, and her last short-lived fancy. Perhaps he himself was being unfaithful merely so as to understand better? At the same time it wore the face of their own lovemaking, and was a brutal medicine, not to be repeated. Really, he was no better than Kate – and that brought him closer to her.

He wrote at once to tell Kate what he had done, and awaited her reply with impatience. It came by return of post.

'What nonsense!' she said. 'I'll have something to say about this! Stop it at once: nothing happened on the terrace, it was just your imagination. Come.'

A separate note from Jules confirmed what she said: 'No, nothing happened.'

Re-reading Kate's last letters, Jim no longer found them so disturbing. He hurried back to her – after all, he was the guilty party this time. He found her grievously hurt by what he had done, but she quite understood; she even vouchsafed him, indirectly, a certain professional admiration.

He assumed she'd never revenge herself in the same way again, unless she had quite certain grounds. And yet – wasn't imagination itself a kind of certainty? Or she might simply do it and not tell him.

Once more they started out afresh – and once more their exaltation took them soaring high, like two great birds of prey.

They were always shy on coming together again. Perhaps each was afraid of offering the other only a repetition of past experience. Just as no two cloudy sunrises are ever identical, so they had never found each other the same as the last time.

Another year went by, with visits at intervals from Jim. They were able at last to realize an old project: they spent a fortnight by Lake Lugano, in a charming little *pension* which Jim had noticed twenty years before when travelling with his mother. After a hard winter they found spring there, and after privations, plenty. The light and the climate were a revelation to Kate.

It was bliss to have big trays with hot chocolate, and rolls and butter and jam, brought to their bedside by the Swiss servant after she had drawn the tall curtains and let in the sun.

Jim watched Kate dive from their boat and swim like a

water-sprite. They amused themselves by throwing stones and breaking bottles floating in the water.

Their life with each other was their only concern.

One night Kate hid in a bush and jumped out suddenly, landing with all her weight on Jim's neck. He nearly fainted. They became aware that his heart wasn't all that it had been.

They went for a long walk to the top of a nearby mountain. On the way down Jim felt a sharp pain in his knee, which had been wounded years before. Kate, ravished, gave him her shoulder to lean on.

They rowed over to the Italian shore. On the way back a storm came up from behind the mountain peaks and quickly bore down on them. The rain blinded them, the boat pitched in the short steep waves and shipped water, the lightning crackled. They were using two pairs of oars, hurrying for the shore, with a quarter of an hour's distance still to cover. Presently their oars clashed.

'Go and sit in the stern, Jim,' said Kate, 'bale out the boat and leave this to me.'

Jim rowed well, but Kate even better. He obeyed. The Kate he saw now, with her thin silk blouse sticking to her skin and streaming wet, was entirely absorbed in her job, bending to her oars like a sailor. Her eyes were sparkling. She would have liked the boat to capsize, just to make everything perfect and give her the chance of saving Jim – or of their drowning together.

She got them safely to land.

They went to the Casino and played roulette, separately, each starting with the same amount of money. Jim watched Kate playing – serious, motionless, suddenly inspired by a number. She was drinking in the game the way she inhaled her cigarettes. She won and won, raised her stake and lost everything.

'It was worth it!' she said. 'And what does it matter anyway whether one wins or loses! How are you getting on, Jim?'

'Slightly ahead at the moment.'

'Let's go and drink it, quick!'

Contrary to their habit they had a liqueur, sitting on a café terrace and smoking English cigarettes. They looked out on the town square, alive with ox-carts and all the bustle of a peasant market.

They recalled Jules's first expedition to the South, made while he was still a student. It was a story he told very well. Bicycling along in the rain, the rucksack under his cape turning him into a hunchback, he had come across a group of girls leaving a factory; they had fallen on him, stopped him, and surrounded him in order to touch his hump, because it would bring them luck. The memory of one of them had haunted him, and he had been sorry afterwards that he hadn't stayed in that town, to see more of her. How funny and charming he must have been just then, their Jules!

They promised themselves a real Italian journey one day, and this consoled them for the fact that their fortnight had come to an end.

Some months later they met again in Venice.

They went into a large church where a troupe of choirboys, dressed in brilliant colours, were singing the litanies of the Saints at the tops of their voices. There was a whole crowd of saints whose names Kate and Jim had never heard before. From time to time the choir sang, in chorus, '*E tutti i Santi del Paradiso*', with an intonation which made Jim think of the first Italian sentence he had heard with Jules, when they disembarked at Naples on their way to Athens; a little child had said, '*O già mangiato la farinata*' ('I've eaten my pudding already'). This song of paradise was the gateway to the long holiday lying before them.

Venice was for them what it has been for so many others, an inexhaustible setting for love; a plaything full of noble yesterdays and the swarming vitality of today. They had an excellent *letto matrimoniale* (double bed) with a roomy mosquito-net. At the bridge corners they crunched little octopuses in vinegar, the size of plums. They were ravished by the popular theatre and its audiences' hilarious response to the crudest of jokes. They glided about on the canals, at random, on the lookout for anything special.

After ten days or so they felt a need to stand back from Venice and experience it from a distance, so they boarded the little steamer at the Riva degli Schiavoni and made a dawdling exploration of the calm lagoon. The flatness and the horizons exalted them. They went to see Chioggia, and were struck to see babies squirming and kicking in their mothers' arms with their eyes covered in flies; the mothers never drove the flies away, yet the eyes of the boys and girls in that town were exceptionally beautiful.

They settled in the one and only inn of a little fishing port, an hour's walk from the Lido, which they visited on foot. Their big white room with its two beds was clean. They lived on spaghetti and tomatoes, like the fishermen.

On the Lido they hired a tent; they were surrounded by Venetian families with quantities of children, the sand was burning hot to the soles of their feet, and they bathed three times a day. Kate improved Jim's diving a little.

They spent their time on the beach, where the grown-up bathers lay on the sand and browned themselves in the sun, as if they had nothing else to do on this earth. Some of them, the blondes especially, were as dark as chocolate. Bronzed young men practised acrobatics. It was all so different from a Northern beach; more showing-off, much bolder sex-appeal, no formality. It was a place of bars and pleasure-lovers; Kate, blonde and tanned like the rest, could have made a hit there if she'd wanted.

And in fact, without meaning to, she was. She had a swimmer's shoulders and was elegantly muscled; she moved neatly, dived beautifully, swam far out to sea; she caught everyone's eyes. Only a dark, powerfully built woman, the empress of the whole beach, could have beaten her over short distances. There was talk of having competitions, but Kate held herself aloof.

Bit by bit, Jim felt himself regarded as the odd man out and Kate as a treasure beyond his deserving, since he neither swam well nor was living it up. His prowess as a boxer and a thrower found no opening here. He was a prince consort. These men were handsomer and gayer than he and Jules; surely, then, they had a better right to Kate? If he absented himself for a minute he found little intrigues springing up, devices for getting into conversation with her.

One afternoon Kate swam out, and it quickly became clear that she was heading for one of the most distant sandbanks. A young giant with glistening black hair jumped up, dashed into the sea and swam after her. To Jim he was like the negro in the ballet of *Scheherazade*. Everyone's eyes were on them. Kate didn't realize she was being followed. He was gaining on her. They swam till they could no longer be seen, even through Jim's marine binoculars. After a long time he picked them up again, two tiny figures emerging from the water and sitting down together on the sandbank. He feared the worst. They must be chatting. The man stood up and seemed to be making some demonstration of feeling. He was the first to start swimming back.

When he landed he was surrounded and questioned. He had big dark eyes and a red mouth. He made a slight gesture with his head in the direction of Jim, rolled in the sand to get dry, and led the others off to the bar.

Through his binoculars Jim could see Kate coming in, swim-

ming steadily; she was a little dark under the eyes. He was there
to receive her at the water's edge, and handed her her wrap.

She told him what had happened:

'When I'd got three quarters of the way I was surprised to
hear a man's voice behind me, and then to see him draw level.
He made a few jokes and tried to grab me; he said he wanted to
help me along. I said, 'No, thanks', quite quietly; however, he did
put his arm round me. My slight knowledge of ju-jitsu was a
help; I broke loose without getting cross. When we landed on
the shoal I was a bit frightened; I was a featherweight compared
to him, and he seemed pretty determined. Still, he couldn't get
anywhere unless I panicked completely or gave in. I was friendly,
but a bit distant, and criticised his swimming. He got up and
began demonstrating his breaststroke, so you couldn't help seeing
his excitement. I pretended not to notice anything, and said the
standard of swimming was much higher in my own country. And
then – well, I got away with it.'

Jim lamented his inability to swim out there after her. He
asked:

'Weren't you interested in him – a handsome man, and in these
surroundings too?'

'Yes,' she said. 'As interested as you'd have been in the tall dark
girl, if she'd dangled herself in front of you in the same surroundings – as much and no more.'

'But there's no reason why she should ever want me.'

'You know nothing about that, it's her affair, not yours. Look,
Jim, my kingdom is the water, yours is elsewhere.'

She saw he was looking anxious:

'He might have tempted me at one time . . . But all that's just
a tasty dish, it's not what I'm after.'

She added, 'We've seen enough of this nest of swimmers. I
shall bathe somewhere else.' And yet Kate would probably have
won the women's race from one island to the other and back,

which had just been announced, and it would have been fun for her. Jim was robbing her of a treat.

They came back to Venice sometimes for the day, if only because they enjoyed gliding gently across the lagoon on the absurdly puffing *vaporetto*.

In the Piazza di San Marco Kate ate a scented ice which didn't agree with her. While they were still in town she was taken with a violent stomach-ache. She had to go into a café, and then to a hotel and even to several private houses, before she had finished being sick. Her head was swimming and her forehead was beaded with perspiration. Sometimes Jim supported her whole weight, which seemed to him smaller than usual that day. She did everything thoroughly, even being sick. He took her to the little steamer and she was sick again, on the deck; supported by Jim's arms, she said: 'You see, you're very good at helping me, Jim, and you do it so nicely that I even share my bilious attack with you.'

In their big room, in the crushing heat of summer which makes clothes impossible, they had nothing to do but talk and make love. Perhaps they did too much of both; perhaps they never could resist the prospect of an unbroken stretch of enjoyment; and perhaps the torrid heat was beginning to make them anaemic. They felt a mounting anxiety, that neither the splendour of the maritime landscape, nor their outings in Venice, could appease. Once Kate mentioned Gilberte.

One evening they went down to the harbour and lay on the grass, where it came just level with the top of the jetty. In the narrow boats nearby the fishermen were peacefully lighting small wood fires and cooking their spaghetti. The sunset died and the stars came out.

'Jim, if you like,' said Kate, breaking the silence between them, 'we could go back to Jules and the children. And then we could all go to the Baltic together. I don't feel at home here, I need the North. I love my Prussia, and you're beginning to love it too. You know I love France, wholeheartedly. In both those countries we're more at home.'

'Certainly,' said Jim. 'Tomorrow, if you like, Kate.'

They went North as joyfully as they had come South. In the train Kate drew caricatures of Jim, with captions that doubled him up with laughter. How well she knew her Jim!

In the first buffet they stopped at in Kate's country, they were astonished to find how high the price of a cup of tea had risen. Inflation was still raging. A very old waiter, suddenly defeated by his bills, began crying and then uttering threats in a mounting fury. He had gone mad and was taken away.

This same inflation also permitted them to take a sleeper together for the first time, and to get home quicker to Jules and the children.

# 4

## An Island in the Baltic

They found the others at home. The holidays were nearly over, but the children would now have fresh ones because Mummy had come back.

'You see, I was right,' Lisbeth said, 'I told you she would!'

'Yes,' said Martine, 'but,' quoting her mother, 'no one's ever right for long.'

Except for Jules, who had to stay behind and work, they all went off to a fishing village on an island in the Baltic. The light was everything Kate had said it would be, and Jim could understand her home-sickness. The fishermen were very different from those in Venice, but just as full of jokes. Their eyes were a startling bright blue.

Kate had an official document which needed renewing. She went with Jim to the mayor's office, where they took down her description all over again: 'Face: *oval*,' dictated the clerk, scrutinizing Kate. 'Hair: *blonde*. Eyes – ' he hesitated a moment and finally decided, '*grey*.'

In these parts, Kate's proverbially blue eyes were, by comparison, grey! She thought of protesting but gave up the idea.

They spent days with Lisbeth and Martine, all with their clothes off, on the dunes. They lived on fish, fresh or smoked. They played tennis on an old, run-down court. Kate was demoniacal in defence, and Jim loved being faced by her furious determination; he always beat her in the end, then carried her off the court in triumph. At ping-pong it was she who won.

They went out sailing at night, in a heavy boat handled by Kate. She taught Jim to steer, and to keep his eye on the star he was steering by when he was tacking. The old sailor with them sat and smoked, not needing to do anything till they came up to the mole again. The island was narrow and the sea was nowhere far away. They liked the life so much that they wanted to buy a house there.

Kate bought a plot of ground covered with pines. Jim was paid some money which he hadn't been expecting till later. They all sat down together to start planning the house.

It would be shallow from back to front, so as to let in the sun everywhere, and high so as to overlook the pines; everyone would have his own small bedroom, fitted up like a ship's cabin; Kate's and Jim's would be double the size of the rest, and so would the communal living-room. Jules would live on the ground floor.

An architect of the modern school, interested by the clear, precise problems of detailed planning submitted to him by Kate, made his sketches. The whole house was to be like a ship. Kate sent for the builder and the carpenter, who seemed to understand what she wanted.

At this point Jim was summoned by a cable from New York to a meeting in Paris. He had to leave.

Kate sent her family home and remained on the spot to oversee the building. The snow came, but at Christmas she was able to celebrate with the workmen; the main part of the job was done. It was only a matter of waiting till spring to finish it off.

She had had a difficult time, and Jim received accounts of various tricky moments.

An American couple, Jack and Micheline, had summoned Jim

to Paris to work with them on their remarkable collection of modern manuscripts.

After Jules, Jack was the friend whose character Jim esteemed most. He was a leader to his fingertips, determined to be fair and always deciding in favour of the other person if there was any doubt.

Jack and Jim teamed up for one or two months, dividing their time between hunting for manuscripts and playing golf; during the day they were never apart. Jack was ten years younger than Jim.

Micheline was young, strikingly beautiful and very much in love with her husband. He wasn't as strong as he looked, and she had to keep a watchful eye on his health.

Jim gradually became aware that complete union between them was a rare occurrence, because it told heavily on Jack's strength and even made him bad-tempered with Micheline.

They lived in a perpetual torment of Tantalus, and it was the purpose of their collection to distract them. They liked Jim to be there all the time, and treated him as a brother.

These two people loved one another yet were unable to make love when they felt like it. The tempestuous, infinitely varied delights of conjugal life were denied them. To start with, Jim had taken care to give them chances of being alone together, and he had made sure, without being asked, that their sleeping-compartments on the train were next to one another. But when he saw the results he began to protect them against themselves, even spending the evening in Jack's room when they were travelling, and there was work to be done on the collection.

His friends took him – to Venice, of all places.

Venice at the off-season, when the days were short, Venice without Kate; it was hard on Jim.

Jack said, 'If you've got a lady-friend, invite her to come along: it's better being four than three.'

'Sure,' said Micheline, with an understanding smile.

Jim's fingers were itching to scribble a telegram to Kate; but their happiness together sometimes made people turn and stare, and he could picture the wounding effect this would have on the more tenuous happiness of Jack and Micheline, and he refrained.

In Venice they stayed at an hotel so exclusive that Kate and he hadn't even been able to have coffee there. What impression would Kate have created in this dining-room full of Anglo-Saxon women in low-cut dresses? In his mind's eye he was superimposing Kate's image on all this. She, and Micheline too, had finer shoulders than any other woman here. Her bearing was as impeccable as Micheline's, and yet she somehow forced attention to focus on her.

Jim thought of inviting Jules to come; his friends would have liked him as much as they would Kate. But Jules wouldn't have been happy in this atmosphere of busy luxury.

Venice, like sleeping-cars, brought Jack and Micheline together too much; Jack had bouts of miserable depression as a result, and these hit Micheline on the rebound. Jim could see this happening; he also understood that, *mutatis mutandis*, he was in the same case as Jack and perhaps as all other men: they were all straws in the blazing fire of their women's beauty. He himself was incapable of living for months at a time in close contact with Kate, it always brought him into a state of exhaustion and involuntary recoil which was the cause of their disasters; they were happier seeing each other at intervals. Even an hour of letting themselves go was too much for Jack and Micheline.

There was less in common between this adoring pair than there was between Kate and him. By watching them, Jim was learning new things both about Kate and himself.

They dawdled their way down Italy by car as far as Rome, acquiring a few precious manuscripts. They were delighted by the

Pantheon, like a round eye looking up to heaven, and by the Villa whose fountains flow in such incredible profusion; and Micheline was particularly sweet to Jack.

They came back to Paris. Jim wanted to show Jack to Kate, and Kate to Jack. He made inquiries about the German collections and managed to discover sufficient grounds for a brief trip to Berlin. Micheline was sitting for a portrait and stayed in Paris.

Jim introduced Kate and Jack at a quiet lunch party. The encounter was an instant success. Kate and Jack paid each other complete attention and neither interrupted the other (this was unusual in both of them). Though they argued over everything, it was in play, and whenever they did happen to agree they laughed with surprise. Their tactics in life were the same: if there is to be war, strike first, unexpectedly, and hard. Be more generous than the generous, don't put up with the mediocre, and as for the riffraff, stamp on them. Egged on by each other they gave examples. Jim was amused, and wondered why these two gave him their friendship. Did he, as they did, belong to the pirate breed? Or was he just an idler, but so good-natured a one that they gave him their favour?

Kate took them into her drawing-room. There was a book by a contemporary author in a luxury edition lying on the table. Jack opened the book and in his large handwriting wrote across the flyleaf the reason why he thought it bad, and signed his name. Doubtless he was autographing it, as an act of friendship. He said to Kate:

'I've written in your book.'

'It isn't mine,' said Kate, 'it was lent to me.'

Jack burst out laughing:

'That's a good one! Why didn't you stop me?'

'Because you'd got launched on doing it.'

Kate told Jim:

'Jack would have made a big impression on me if I'd met him when I was a girl.'

Jack made the same observation on his own side.

'Why does this give me so much pleasure?' Jim wondered.

When the train left, Kate gave them each, through the window, one of the two orchids she was holding in her hand. Jack kept his, but before they reached Paris he gave it to Jim, in case Micheline might be worried about it.

They went to see Micheline's portrait. It had her special expression 'for Jack', and he was shocked that she had been able to put it on in front of the painter.

They left.

Jim was sent to America for five months on business. He and Kate exchanged untroubled letters. He looked up some of his old girlfriends and could have collected some new ones; but he was faithful to Kate, and hoped she was being faithful too.

## 5

## *The Dream Room*

When Jim came back Kate had settled on her own in Paris, in a single room. She was studying the prospects for her career as a painter and designer. Her earnings were now as important to the family as those of Jules. She took it seriously, and bore as much resentment as gratitude towards Jim for having caused her to embark on it.

Jim was glad she was a painter, but sometimes found it disconcerting and almost irritating.

The simplicity of Kate's life, the way she dressed, the sense of order she brought to her work, were both touching and surprising to Jim. She was no longer the queen bee surrounded by her court; for a time, at any rate, she was a worker.

They were reserved with each other at first, as usual, but were soon on close terms.

Kate came to live not far from Jim's mother's flat, where he had his study and bedroom. He spent most of his nights with Kate.

Jim introduced her to some fashionable Parisian ladies. She was still wearing a soberly cut black dress, beautiful to Jim but provincial in the eyes of others. She promptly began dressing in the fashion, and Jim was sorry.

She was now settled permanently in the same city as he, and was working there, as he did. It was a new era, with its own beauties and dangers. They had never seen each other before except in the 'perpetual holiday' setting. But now their working lives were standing face to face.

They made a pilgrimage to the place where Kate had leapt into the Seine.

On Sundays they searched the country districts round Paris for a house for themselves and the family, who were to rejoin them. Several times Jim thought he had found just what they were looking for, but Kate, with infallible instinct, turned it down. It was she who found what they needed for the summer.

The family arrived, all well and in tearing spirits. Kate quickly and deftly moved them in, and their life together began again. Jules had some long books to translate and often needed Jim's help.

Jim kept his social relations and his visits to Paris down to a minimum. He nevertheless had a clash with Kate one morning when they woke up; she accused him of frittering away his time and energies and not concentrating them sufficiently on her. They were on edge from overwork and agreed to have a holiday from each other, but it only lasted a few hours.

There was a billiard table in the house. They played after dinner, with Jules, who had a comic style of his own.

Kate gave piano lessons to her daughters and also to Jim, but he never got beyond 'Chopsticks'.

Kate had lent Jim a Chinese gold ring in the shape of a whirling dragon. One night she said to him:

'I lent it to Albert too.'

Jim, who was playing with the ring, crushed it between his fingers. Kate, delighted, kept the squashed ring. Jim had it repaired, and it reappeared on Kate's hand.

For the winter Kate found a warmer house. It was in a garden, and they occupied two out of the three storeys. Jules had an enormous study and drawing-room combined, on the ground floor, with a long, massive table for his manuscripts and bulky dictionaries. He got up early and spent the whole day in there; in the evening, blinking from fatigue, he would ask the indignant Kate to excuse him and let him go to bed.

The furniture was old but had been well looked after. The rooms were small, except for Jules's study and Kate's bedroom.

The latter had furniture of carved oak almost honey-yellow in patches, and a four-poster with an oak canopy. Little rugs, dotted here and there, skidded on the well-polished floor. In front of one of the windows there was an aged twisted paulownia; Jim used to lie across the bed, with his head hanging over the edge, and gaze at its leaves the wrong way up.

All this was clean contrary to their tastes; yet, after a fortnight they christened this bedroom 'the dream room' because it made them so welcome, and because it gave them night after night of deep, peaceful sleep. In the light of the autumn sunset the oak wardrobe glowed red.

Mathilde, who had never been out of Germany, was surprised to find how easy it was to get used to French ways. People lied more readily in France, according to her, and were more given to exaggeration, but once you knew how much to allow for this it was all right. She made a number of friends in town, though she found them too eloquent and flowery. She and the girls slept in a room near Kate's, and Jules had a comfortable sofa-bed in his study.

They were well anchored here, and, as things turned out, stayed for two years. The dream room lived up to its name for a year and eight months – which is a long time. Kate's honeyed fragrance married up with the honey-colour of the old oak. Their deep sleep was a thank-offering to the Creator.

The girls quickly learnt French and had various successes at school.

Was there still any latent disturbance anywhere? If so, it appeared to have been laid to rest.

Jim's mother was away travelling. Jim invited Kate to spend a day in his half of the flat. It was a strange experience for him to have Kate in this sanctuary; the atmosphere was so full of his mother's presence, and she was so much against the life he led with Kate.

She and Kate were two of a pair, equally independent and uncompromising. But his mother had been married for only two years and had remained faithful to his father's memory; she lived then with her books, her thoughts and visits from friends. She considered Jim a weak character who had dissipated his talents.

Jim showed Kate his mother's bedroom and drawing-room, but they spent no time in her part of the flat.

They went to a music-hall one evening. Half-way through the show Kate said:

'Stay here. It's too hot, I'm going out for a breath of air.'

She was a long time. Jim began getting anxious. A programme-seller came up to him and said,

'Sir, you're wanted outside.'

'Who wants me?'

'It's about the lady.'

He went out, following the programme-seller along the corridors whose deep carpets made electric sparks if you dragged your feet. He found Kate lying on her back on the floor, her face streaming with blood from a long cut on her forehead. He thought she'd been murdered. Who by?

A man whom he hadn't noticed introduced himself:

'I'm the doctor on duty. The lady must have fainted and fallen against this radiator. I've examined the wound, I don't think it's very deep, but she must be taken to hospital. She came round and was able to say where your seat was and give a description of you.'

Jim tried to carry Kate, but his heart suddenly faltered. A burly stage-hand took her in his arms, as if she had been a big doll, and carried her to a taxi. A drop of blood fell at every step.

'How quickly it happens!' thought Jim. 'It was just the same with the engine. This page-boy beauty, powdered and curled, my Kate – and now this slaughtered carcass.'

The stage-hand refused the note he held out, and wished them good luck.

The taxi took them to the Hôpital Beaujon. Kate was carried into the casualty ward and laid on the operating table.

'Nothing broken,' said the house-physician, 'not even her nose. A big cut on the forehead, we'll have to stitch that. The bleeding's nothing. Leave the room, please.'

Jim waited; the door opened a little after half an hour and he heard a voice say, 'Give her a stiff tot . . . Yes, she can be looked after at home, she's quite fit to be moved.'

They gave him a Kate who lurched as she walked, with an enormous cotton-wool bonnet round her head and a cross-shaped dressing over her face. Her eyes, undamaged, opened.

In the taxi a desolate voice spoke from the bonnet:

'She won't be disfigured – not disfigured – that's what they said – the doctors – but she may be fairly ugly all the same.'

Jim hadn't thought of that; he had simply been terrified she would die. He burst out laughing. He kissed the towering bonnet, which began laughing too from under its dressings, and sobbed at the same time.

How had Kate managed to fall like that, inertly – she who was so deft in all she did, who moved with a dancer's precision?

Jim learnt to change the dressings. The big snowy turban suited Kate. The lumpy swellings slowly went down. After two months all there was left was a sort of whitish sabre-cut, and a bizarre memory, half-way between the Ballets Russes and a whodunit.

\*

In the spring Kate and Jim went on an expedition to find a seaside place for the summer holidays, and made an impromptu trip for a week to the Ile d'Oléron.

They stayed in a bare attic containing a sagging double bed with three straw mattresses, and a rough wooden crucifix. They explored the whole island but always came back to its wilder side.

One foggy evening Kate wanted another swim in the Atlantic, which was calm that day.

Jim didn't like her swimming out alone at night; there were currents. She promised not to be long, and to come ashore at the same place as she went in.

He paced up and down, carrying Kate's skirt and blouse over his arm and gradually becoming vexed because she was having such a long bathe.

No doubt she was enjoying herself in the water. But surely she always behaved like this on purpose, so as to frighten those who loved her and treat herself to the sight of their distress? It always worked with Jules, who by this time would already have started calling to her; but Jim considered she oughtn't to have tried it on him too, because he never tried to restrict her fantasies. The fog was getting thicker and night had fallen. He imagined her with sense of direction lost, swimming in the darkness, exhausted, sinking.

At least half an hour had passed. Jim had thoughts of going to the village and rousing the fishermen – but what was the use on such a thick night?

Perhaps Kate was on the reef, waiting for daylight? Perhaps her body would be found washed up on the shore? The tide was going out and Jim followed it down; he called, but his voice was drowned by the waves.

He decided to leave the shore, and walked a hundred yards towards the woods. The whole thing was too stupid! He yelled a curse at Kate at the top of his voice.

He heard a pattering of bare feet and a quavering voice swearing back at him. It was Kate!

She came up to him. She had come ashore near her starting-point and had passed close to him but hadn't seen him in the fog, and had been looking for him further up, facing the woods, while he had been waiting for her behind her back, facing the ocean. She was icy cold, and was convinced that Jim, for a joke, had been trying to make her go back to the village naked!

She flung herself on his neck. They didn't laugh about it till the next day.

They suddenly wanted to visit the coast of the Landes.

They took the night train from Paris and at dawn reached a small town on the bay of Arcachon. They were hungry. An oyster-woman was laying out her small, succulent oysters. They ate dozen upon dozen, washing them down with a light white wine which seemed quite harmless. Kate, thirsty, for once drank more than Jim.

'Go steady on the wine, Kate.'

'Don't worry, Jim.'

With their packs on their backs they set out through the town. Kate began singing loudly. It was nice to hear, but it woke people up; Jim told her so and she thanked him sincerely, but began again a moment later.

They got out into the country, to the house of a customs official to whom they had a letter of introduction.

'Would the little lady like to rest a minute in an armchair?' said the official's wife, opening the door of their large, tidy bedroom.

Kate accepted.

Jim discussed the countryside with the friendly couple, in their dining-room. The time came to leave, and the wife knocked several times on her bedroom door; no answer. She went in but checked herself, round-eyed: Kate, her neatly folded clothes piled on a chair, was sleeping the sleep of the just, snuggling naked in the conjugal bed.

They didn't wake her. The customs official's wife invited Kate and Jim to lunch. It was a merry meal. Kate explained that she had felt giddy and couldn't understand where she was. The man and his wife were proud of the effects of the local wine.

Kate and Jim trudged on along a soft, sandy track, through pines with notched trunks, till they came to a pair of huts joined together. A large family of resin-gatherers lived there. One of the huts had been built for a friend of Jim's, and had been lent to them. A few stars could be glimpsed through the roof but the rain didn't come in.

The next day they went out shooting migrant thrushes, and Kate learnt to shoot them sitting. They dropped like ripe plums. To go shooting together was a new pleasure, and the only meat they had was whatever game they brought back.

With some resin-gatherers they went after ringdoves. Crouching in a hide dug in the sand and covered with pine-branches, they pulled strings which caused a fluttering of wings among captive doves tethered to boards in the nearby treetops. Flocks of wild doves came down to settle and at a given signal all the guns fired together. Kate and Jim soon tired of it, finding it too easy, and they preferred staying outside, on a wooden bench, shooting at sparrowhawks which came swooping down at the decoys. That at least was shooting, even when you missed.

The evenings were cold; they stripped off their clothes and roasted themselves in front of a big fire of pine-faggots.

They explored in all directions. The great dunes were over three hundred feet high, so vast that you could make-believe you were in the Sahara. On the deserted shore they spent whole days naked. Sometimes they took turns to bury each other in the hot sand, with a little paper funnel in each nostril for breathing through; nothing stuck out except these funnels, and sometimes a pair of nipples. They built a temple with driftwood and the skeletons of birds.

They saw themselves as Adam and Eve.

They lost their way in the endless, unvarying forest, and after wandering helplessly for hours were obliged to blow the ox-horn which the resin-gatherers had given them for just such an emergency. They had taken it out of politeness, believing it quite unnecessary. Unfortunately, they hadn't been taught what call to make, and the one they invented, and sounded till they were out of breath, bore a chance resemblance to the call for 'forest fire'. Men ran up from round about, took them for practical jokers and tried to march them off to gaol. They were saved by the arrival of their resin-gathering friends.

When they went home they had great fun at table telling the story of their adventures, and showing off the curious pipe they had bought for Jules, and sets of shells – pink for the girls, black for Mathilde.

One sunny morning Jim rose early and went into the garden. On a worm-eaten wooden post he noticed a tiny greenish patch which appeared to be changing its shape. He looked at it from close up. It was a hemisphere, the size of a small shot, alternately spreading out and contracting with perfect unanimity, like a covey of partridges which by turns takes wing or squats flat. Spiders? Greenfly? A little bird was pecking assiduously at a neighbouring post; was it feeding on similar tiny hemispheres? Jim put his eye closer. The little ball spread out wider and became invisible on the lichen-covered surface. What was the signal for these movements? Jim's feelings were stirred; and this little ball stayed in his memory as the symbol of their household, controlled at all times by Kate's guiding instinct.

*

The girls were sitting on the grass with Jim.

'Jim,' said Martine, 'what do people do after they're dead?'

'She means,' explained Lisbeth, 'what do souls do?'

'They come out of people's bodies, just as the dragonfly came out of its larva the other day,' said Jim.

'Yes,' said Martine, 'they dry their wings.'

'They get together with other souls,' Jim went on, 'and then suddenly, whish! they all migrate together, like eels – only they go to the moon.'

'What do they do there?' said Lisbeth.

'They think things over, and then one fine day they set off again – to fiery planets, and icy planets, and other kinds of planets too.'

'I like it best when they change from one kind of animal to another,' said Martine.

'That's all right while they're still on the earth. But after that, they go soaring up among the myriads of stars, into the Milky Way, and play hide-and-seek with God.'

'Do they find him?' asked Martine.

'Nobody knows for certain,' said Jim. 'The great thing is to join in the game.'

'Ah, yes!' said Martine.

'No,' said Lisbeth.

'And what about Mummy?' asked Martine.

'Mummy always catches you in the end,' said Jim.

The next day Kate appeared, in a high state of enthusiasm, brandishing a book which had just come out. 'At last,' she said, 'here's a man saying out loud the very thing I'm always thinking to myself: the sky we see above us is a hollow ball, no bigger than that. We're walking upright, with our heads pointing to its centre. There's an outward-going pull, under our feet, in the direction of the solid crust inside which this bubble is encased.'

'How thick is the crust?' said Jim. 'And what is there on the other side of it?'

'Oh, go and have a look, Jim,' said Kate. 'What's on the other side, indeed! What a question to ask among gentlemen!'

They all laughed.

Time was flowing, flowing . . . Happiness isn't easy to record. And it wears out; and nobody notices . . .

It was a great family event when Jim could afford to give Kate a small car, a saloon with blue-and brown-tartan upholstery. Kate quickly learnt to drive. It was only a three-seater, but Kate stuffed her whole flock into it and took them out for picnics. She drove Jim into Paris in the morning and brought him back at night; a great improvement on the trams, which were too few and too full. Sometimes the whole family, including Mathilde, would set to and clean the car; they loved it like a faithful dog, and invented legends about it. Jim made up a story for the girls, in which the little car saved Kate's life after following her along the street, with nobody driving it.

Jim went to Greece, where he missed Jules. He didn't revisit *the smile*; why should he? He had the original. On his way back he sent for Kate to join him on the Riviera. She got there in two days by means of forced marches in the little car, and they toured half France, taking their time. Jim was driving this time, and it was in his hands that the car gave up the ghost. Kate, rightly, sided with the car and against Jim. Repairs took a long time, and they went walking meanwhile in the Pyrenees.

At a spa, practically deserted during this part of the season, Kate, out of curiosity, tried the hot springs. Jim came to join her in a room full of steam but nevertheless cold and draughty. He noticed one of the window-panes was missing.

'It doesn't matter,' said Kate, shivering, 'I thought at first it was on purpose, and anyway I never catch cold. But in my country the nurse who told me to stay in here for a quarter of an hour would get punished; anyone who was really ill wouldn't have come out again.'

While they waited for the car to be done they read the remarks of an anonymous columnist in the back numbers of a provincial newspaper, and collected quotations from it.

They started out again.

Carcassonne they found bogus and depressing, but they discovered several little fortified towns whose unspoiled beauty was pleasing.

A shadow passed over them from time to time. Jim sometimes felt Kate was inconsiderate towards others; when he said, 'One mustn't hurt people,' she detected a possible allusion to Gilberte, and retorted:

'On the contrary. All the way through life you've got to be like a surgeon: see things coming and take prompt action.'

Back to Paris.

Echoes of their disagreements came to Jules. He told them a Hindu tale:

'There were two lovers, tormented by love and jealousy. They attained the height of felicity together; and they ruined it. Several times they parted and came together again and found themselves each time more in love than before. But they went on hurting one another, and parted for good. Years later the man, heartbroken, longed to see his sweetheart again before he died. He set out in search of her, confident that wherever she might be her beauty would have made her famous. When he found her she was the star of a company of dancing-girls of easy morals. He approached her; gazed at her and could find nothing to say; tears ran from his eyes. He followed the company on its travels and watched his love dancing and smiling for other men. He held nothing against her, he only wanted to be able to look at her. "At last," she said to him, "you really love me."'

They commented on this story in their different ways. Kate said the girl was right. Jim thought of Manon Lescaut and Des Grieux.

Jules told Kate:

'Your maxim is that in a couple at least one party must be faithful – the other.'

He also said:

'If you love somebody you love him as he is. You don't want to influence him, because then he wouldn't be the same person any more. It's better to give up the person you love than to try and change him, whether by kindness or by domination.'

Jim wanted to die of his love for Kate. To survive was an offence. Male spiders know it – and so do their females.

And when there has been one offence, others inevitably follow.

# 6

## *Paul*

After several weeks of fine weather there comes a stormy spell, for no apparent reason. You're still dazzled by the sun – and yet the month has been spoiled, and the season, and perhaps the year.

(Provincial paper)

Kate was sitting behind Jim, who was at the wheel of their car. She suddenly made an allusion to Gilberte; he didn't reply. He spoke, and she in her turn said nothing. They were trundling smoothly through the Bois de Boulogne. He thought she was tired and wanted to think and he respected her silence, devoting his attention to picking a pleasant route for their drive.

He could see a little of her in the driving mirror. She leaned forward and took his heavy walking-stick. He felt a threat building up behind him. Her hands moved. He foresaw the blow, which landed with all the force Kate could impart to it in such a confined space, on his ear, as he was in the act of ducking. He thought he could feel blood, but when he touched the spot his fingers came away dry. Dazed, he grabbed the stick and she let go.

'Oh, Kate!' he said.

She had taken his silence as an insult and resolved to bring it to an end.

*

'Oh, when,' she said to him one day – 'when are you going to stop giving me bits of yourself and give me everything?'

'Oh, when,' said Jim, 'when are you going to let our love flow quietly along its appointed course, instead of slicing it off short, the way the baker cuts his dough?'

A young man made his appearance in Kate's life, like some large, unknown insect falling on to a balcony.

She told Jules and Jim about him.

She had met him one day when she was out shopping with Mathilde. He had followed them for nearly an hour, politely coming after them into shops and looking calmly at Kate each time he got the chance, and also at Mathilde.

On the second occasion, Kate was alone. He had introduced himself to her respectfully but without embarrassment, saying he would like to talk to her. Kate was intrigued by his serious manner, and consented to drink tea with him in a *pâtisserie*. He was tall, correct, distinguished, and keen on his work as an architect. He thought that the world was unnecessarily complicated and that humanity used its time unintelligently. He wanted order, clarity, new values. He fancied that Kate's bearing, her determination, her style of dress, matched his own aspirations.

Jules and Jim decided he was right: Kate's archaic smile contained an implicit judgement on the present age.

Kate saw him again, and told them. He had a young wife, tall and slender like himself, who didn't share his zeal for reform. They were nudists and fervent swimmers. They had no children.

From what they heard, Jules and Jim thought they would like him; but they had a foreboding that Paul (as his name was) would be exploited as a lever by Kate. She had been piling up grievances; an avalanche was threatening. The Albert–Harold period might be coming back, with variations.

Kate slowly roused up Jim's anxiety. Paul considered the curve of Kate's calves to be symbolic. Had he touched them?

Jim wanted to meet Paul. It seemed the desire was mutual. The introduction took place in a café. Kate was at ease, and the two men almost so. Paul was just as Kate had described. He did nothing to draw attention; at the same time he looked capable of seeking inspiration from Kate in a way which would please neither his wife nor Jim – and of doing it impassively, practically under their noses.

Jim had made up his mind to let things take whatever course they would. With his heart and hands he maintained a little kerb, as it were, round Kate, lest she stray by accident; but he wasn't going to raise it to the height of a wall.

Jules thought, 'Well, we might have got someone much worse.'

Jim remembered something Jules had once said to Kate: 'Every summer you take another of my friends as your lover.'

But she had discovered Paul by herself.

The fault lay with Jules and Jim: they weren't all that she needed.

One evening Kate and Jim dressed carefully, took the little car and had dinner in town. For once they ate highly seasoned dishes and drank wine.

They went to an arena, where they joined Paul and his wife to see a famous negro boxer. His opponent was a thickset, dogged little Englishman. The negro, for all his skill, only beat him on points and never put him on the canvas. The crowd were disappointed.

At a café afterwards, Paul's wife turned out to be a lively talker and, as Kate had said, somewhat conservative. Kate took the initiative. Paul was pleasant and quiet.

Jim was on the alert; and yet, perhaps, less observant of Kate's needs than she would have wished. She always liked the man with her to be extremely attentive.

They drove home as fast as their little car would go, and, as usual, had their bath together.

What came over them now? What were they being punished for? The stimulating food they had eaten? Or their animal response to the boxing?

Kate was naked, and Jim, as he often did, took her in his arms to put her gently on to her back and kiss her. She resisted. Was Jim forcing the pace and taking her consent for granted? The ambiguities of their evening with the other two had left Kate on edge. She felt she was being degraded, and repulsed Jim violently. He saw her face contorting with rage. She seized an electric iron to throw at him. They were in danger of hurting each other in this narrow bathroom. Jim had to act fast; with the flat of his hand he dealt her a volley of rapid blows on the face, so as to confuse but not harm her. She fell backwards through the door into their dream room. Lurching forward, Jim jumped over her and collapsed on to the bed, with a hand on his heart. Kate, frightened, ran to him and put her arms round him. They lay there in silence, throbbing with emotion, and gradually their breathing became quieter. They fell asleep.

Kate stayed in bed the next morning, and Jim with her. Her face was hardly marked; she told the children she had fallen down, but Mathilde glanced suspiciously at Jim.

Once again their turbulent love took possession of them, but now this love had two *banderillas* sticking into its neck: Gilberte and Paul.

Jim had never stopped seeing Gilberte, and Kate was still seeing Paul.

Jim stuck to his dogma: 'Gilberte equals Jules; let's accept the fact and be happy.' And Kate had found a new one: 'Gilberte equals Paul.'

How much did Paul mean to her? Jim racked his brains but had no hope of guessing the answer. Ever since Jim had applied the law of retaliation against her, Kate had told him nothing; and she remained capable of everything. In the art of deception she was so much his superior that he no longer asked her any questions.

Kate thought Jim was taking Paul too calmly; if the problem left him cold, she was free to do as she liked where Paul was concerned!

If this was so, she must take great care to keep Jim's uncertainty up to a satisfying level.

Jim's attitude was that happiness was within their grasp, here in the house – 'and if she can't see it, so much the worse for us! Maybe she's got to have warfare all the time, but I can't take it any more.'

One night, Jim's hand encountered something cold between the mattress and the wooden frame at the end of the bed behind Kate's head. It was the revolver he used to carry in the car. He hid it and said nothing.

Jules wouldn't have defended himself, and that was why Kate never wanted to hit him. In Jules there was peace – which Kate disdained.

Kate started wanting a flat in Paris; it was becoming necessary both for the girls' education and for her work. She found one; Jim's premonition was that they would be less and less happy there, and he even thought of leaving for America; but Kate was so busy and determined that he drifted into staying.

They said good-bye to the dream room, which hadn't been living up to its name so well since Paul appeared.

To furnish their new place they sold their house on the island. They all loved it, even though none of them had seen it, except

Kate. It was a long way off; besides, when would they have the leisure to live in it?

The interior decoration of the flat was designed by Paul – an austere fantasy in which the walls were all different colours, four carefully chosen colours to every room.

# 7

## Stresses and Strains

One day, your scissors, your penknife or your spectacles go astray; they hear your voice and would love to answer, 'Here I am!', but they can't.

(Provincial paper)

They lived there for more than two years.

Jules took a job in his own country and was with them only at intervals – Jules, their protector.

Kate and Jim no longer resolved their conflicts by immediate, spectacular quarrels. Arrears were piling up. They were hopelessly at loggerheads over Gilberte.

Kate lived only three minutes away from Jim's home and five from Gilberte; the hours he spent with Gilberte became more and more obvious, and it was a thorn in Kate's side to feel Gilberte so near. Tacit warfare sprang up between the two women.

Kate took Jim to see a house for the summer holidays, on the Channel coast. They drove all day and arrived in pitch darkness. It was raining and their lights gave out.

They tried to back the car into the small shed that served as a garage, but couldn't manage it. They lit matches, they pushed, but in vain. They exerted themselves as they had done sometimes in the past over a chess problem. It seemed to them that some odd force, a malign spirit, was opposing them. They crawled about, looking for the boundary-stone, paving-stone or whatever else the invisible obstacle might be, but could find nothing. Irritated and depressed they went to bed without supper, discussing the incident and telling each other stories of similar happenings in their childhood, stories which all had some strange outcome. They felt persecuted and said it must be an omen.

They woke late and ran out to the car. One of the rafters of the shed had fallen part-way down and blocked a corner of the entrance at the top; they hadn't groped as high as that.

Jules, the children and Mathilde joined them, and their old gay life began again.

On the first morning, Jim, in addition to various other games, succeeded with Martine as partner in hitting a shuttlecock three hundred times over the garden hedge, in one continuous rally.

At lunchtime a telegram arrived for Kate. She had to return to Paris for twenty-four hours.

'I'm going,' she told Jim – which was as much as to say, 'We're going.'

'Oh!' said Jim; he was tired, and about to have a sleep. 'Is there really any need for me to come?'

'My God!' he thought instantly, aware of what a dreadful thing he had said.

'Have it your own way!' said Kate. 'I'll take Jules and Mathilde, if they'd like it.'

They enjoyed driving with Kate and didn't often get the chance.

Jim realized the full enormity of his offence.

He was two days on his own with Lisbeth and Martine. Before meals he took them for an *apéritif* (a glass of barley-water) on the terrace (which was simply two round tables) of the little café, by the big pond. They watched the behaviour of the ducks and were indignant at the cruelty of the drakes, and exchanged comments in which Jim detected Jules's mind at one moment and Kate's at another. He had a pleasant time but was not quite free from anxiety.

When the three came back, pleased with their trip, they were like a little club; as Kate took care to underline.

Shortly after this she asked Jim if he was planning to go and see Gilberte in the country that autumn as he usually did. When Jim said he was, she sent him packing, though their long seaside holiday had only just begun.

The rest of the hive, not fully informed of the situation, felt vaguely that Jim was at odds with their queen: so it was quite normal for him to go away.

But it was a shattering break for Jim.

Gilberte was very conscious of Kate's presence. Years ago she had given her instant consent to Jim's marrying Kate and having children; but through no action of her own this hadn't happened, and she had begun hoping again. She was unhappy.

So was Jim. He couldn't have given up Gilberte, he would have looked too mean in his own eyes. He had told Kate so from the start, and she had always fiercely resented it. All the good-will and, as he thought, the integrity which he showed in not giving to either what belonged of right to the other, were frustrated by Gilberte's sorrow and Kate's anger. He hadn't lost faith in his dream of the future, but he no longer believed it could be made to come true on this earth.

His love for Kate had shot across the sky of his life like a dazzling comet. Now, he visualized it sometimes as a kite tangled in overhead power-lines. He still said, 'It'll all work out somehow,' but his mother who knew a little of both Gilberte and Kate, said, 'Nothing works out and everything has to be paid for.'

★

Since Kate and he had started taking a rest from each other now and again, by agreement, he had been spending more evenings and nights at his mother's flat, in the bed he had slept in as a student; a neutral port, between Kate and Gilberte.

Jim had a high opinion of his mother. When he was a child she had taught him never to argue; her yes meant yes and her no meant no, and he had felt sorry for his little friends who wasted so much time whining and lamenting in order to get their way with their parents. After his adolescence his mother had had no further influence over him, except possibly to push him in the opposite direction as she always proceeded by fixed principles, and Jim was an experimentalist.

He never wanted to marry any of the girls she chose for him, and she had never approved of any of those he would have enjoyed being married to. The highly adaptable home she always kept open for him had been the cause of his remaining a bachelor. Meals were put out ready for them on trays, and they ate them separately at any time of day, just as it happened to suit them. They worked in their own rooms and visited one another frequently but briefly.

Kate sometimes gave quiet, unpretentious parties in her flat (it was no longer 'their' flat) for German and French painters. Jim felt he was superfluous on these occasions and went to them less and less. He couldn't unreservedly admire Kate except when she was alone; in company, he began making comparisons.

Sleep was still a bond of union between them. But sometimes, in the night, Jim heard Kate's breathing become sibilant and slow and rhythmical, like the bellows at a forge rising and falling. He was worried and he was sorry for her; he knew she was lying awake, caught up in the whirlwind of her thoughts; and he also knew the outcome would be a long, pointless conversation lasting till dawn, and quite possibly leading to a violent outburst from Kate, who would then try to hit him.

She had bought herself a little revolver, which she hid in one place after another, without reference to Jim.

One morning at daybreak, after an argument about Gilberte, an argument carried on in low voices so as not to wake the girls, Kate bounded up from bed, ran to the open window and threw one leg over the edge of the small balcony. Jim saw her naked, in profile, superb, gazing at the void with the little courtyard four storeys below. He had a crazy hope she was going to jump – and he would surely jump after her. Calmed by the cold air, Kate came back to bed.

Spring brought a lull, and for almost a month they knew their old happiness again. They even had hopes of a child. As Kate and Jules had remarried, it would have to bear Jules's surname. 'What of it?' thought Jim, 'these external laws don't matter, and Jules would be as willing as before.' But Kate, who had had a middle-class upbringing (though one wouldn't always have guessed it), couldn't bring herself to accept the prospect.

Jim went travelling in the South of France with a compatriot of Jack's. He thought a great deal about the child and the portrait of it painted by Kate, the little head with its tangle of fair hair and its serious eyes. Once more he was trembling with love for Kate and for the child, whose presence would undo all the harm and solve all their problems. But when he came back the hope of a child had vanished.

'When everything's all right again,' said Kate, 'we'll have one that's really our own.'

But they no longer quite believed it.

Love and indifference swept through them by turns. Indifference was gaining; but love, when it came, still cancelled out everything else.

Kate had said, 'No one ever really loves for more than one single moment.' That moment kept coming back.

'Love is a sanction applied by human beings to one another,' Jules had once said.

Kate had to spend six weeks in her own country, and it was agreed that Jim should drive her. But when he stipulated that he must be away for only five days, she set out alone. And that was another big break between them.

They didn't write to one another.

He thought once more that everything was over.

How fine, how beautiful, to have no marriage certificate, no vows, and to rely from day to day on love alone! But if ever the wind of doubt begins to blow, the world becomes a void.

# 8

## Breaking-point

'. . . Love brought remorse, at first no bigger than a seedling, but now grown into a mighty oak.'

(Provincial paper)

Jim had time to think things over. He had spread distress about him when he had meant to bring only joy. Certainly pioneers were needed, people who ventured along new ways; but they must be humble and selfless. He had been flippant in his attitude to life. He must now demolish, piece by piece, the unhappiness he had caused, and the first debt he must pay was the first he had contracted; his promise to Gilberte that they 'would grow old together' was something he had never forgotten, but he had never assigned a date to it, and he could go on postponing it indefinitely; it was like a forged note. He must therefore promise Gilberte that he would marry her, if she wanted and when she wanted. He no longer had any hope of marrying Kate.

In a novel that Kate had lent him he found a passage marked by her, about a woman on a voyage who gave herself, in imagination, to a man in the next cabin. Jim was struck, as if by a confession; for this was Kate's way of exploring the universe, and was bound to be carried out in practice as well as in thought. He had the same lightning curiosity himself. Perhaps everybody had.

But he controlled his own, for Kate's sake. Whether she controlled hers, for his sake, he was not sure.

Kate came back and for several days didn't summon him; this reinforced his decision. When she did send for him her words and manner were cool. Jim availed himself of the opportunity to tell her, even if only to put her at her ease, what he was thinking of doing for Gilberte.

They were in their car. Kate was driving. At first she seemed not to hear; then she swerved violently. Jim seized the wheel. She said:

'As you've got this idea you must carry it out. Even if you changed your mind I should force you to do it.'

He told her Gilberte wasn't hoping for any immediate change in their lives. He expected Kate to turn sarcastic or violent or to send him away; but she didn't.

She had however said to him some time previously, 'Now that I love you less . . .', which is almost worse than 'Now that I don't love you any more.'

Their future was limited; in the long or the short run they would come to a dead stop. Kate had flirted with *the irreparable*, without ever, she thought, breaking anything; and now Jim was trying the same thing and succeeding at once.

Baffled, they were seeking a refuge; and finding none. Out of habit they took shelter once more in each other, but in desperation, like prisoners under sentence. They had one of their renewals of happiness; better for them if they had died of it!

At night, half asleep, Kate sometimes said: 'Gilberte's not hoping for an immediate change . . .'

She made strenuous efforts to meet Gilberte, with or without Jim. She wrote to Gilberte: calm letters at first, then hectic ones which were a mixture of frankness and scorn.

Jim didn't interfere.

'Let them decide as they please,' he thought, 'I'll do it, whatever it is; even a meeting between the three of us, a clash of two worlds – but at least let them get on with one another, as Jules and I do, so that when one of them smiles I don't feel guilty about the other.'

At night Jim pictured this interview taking place. It was always different; sometimes the two women sided together against him; sometimes, after looking at each other carefully, they understood and accepted each other. But sometimes Kate came to blows with Gilberte, who defended herself.

Jim had a dream, in which the women were two cloudy, elongated forms exchanging flashes of lightning and gliding slowly about like snakes, in a strategy which he couldn't understand.

One evening when he was in bed at his own home, almost asleep, he heard the horn of their car in the distance sounding Kate's customary rhythmical call.

He ran to his balcony. At first he saw nothing; then he distinguished Kate's car driving in and out under the trees on a raised open space reserved for pedestrians, bumping down on to the tarmac again, wandering round the deserted square, mounting the traffic islands and almost colliding with street lamps and bench-seats, like a riderless horse or a phantom ship.

He threw up his arms and shouted at the top of his voice, but in vain. She drove away down a side-turning.

There were no taxis on the rank opposite so he couldn't follow her.

She said nothing about it the next day.

Jules came to Paris for two days, and Kate and Jim, separately, told him what they were suffering. He remembered the time when he had been in love, and refrained from passing judgement now.

He had a big room on the seventh floor but Kate insisted on him taking hers, so as to be near their daughters, while she and Jim went off to sleep at a hotel.

For a short time, floating on a serene tide of happiness, they were able to forget. They didn't ring for the servant on duty, and apart from two rolls which Jim had in his pocket their only food was themselves and their emotions.

This last stronghold of their love came under attack, like all the others.

A friend of Kate's, a woman doctor who was a disciple of Freud, arrived in Paris and saw Kate frequently. She interrogated Kate, using the methods she had learnt. Kate gave her some intimate details of her life with Jim, a breach of confidence which Jim detested. The friend told Kate:

'You mustn't go on like this, you're giving Jim too much of the upper hand.' And she indicated something which needed changing.

Kate told Jim, and the change was made. But though they weren't aware of it the feature in question was something essential, at least to Jim, and though he didn't mean to let the alteration affect him the vital thread of their intimacy was broken.

Their unity was disrupted. It was as if their physical love were a shattered moon, apparently intact, revolving in its usual orbit round the earth, with its two fragments still adhering together but ready to fly apart at the slightest shock.

Jim saw a drawing, by Willette, of a drunkard beating his pretty young wife over the head with an empty bottle. Underneath was a caption: 'Love's a hard thing to kill.'

'Ah, yes,' sighed Jim, 'hard it is, very hard; maybe impossible.'

He remembered a Chinese play in which, as the curtain rose, the Emperor bowed to the public and announced: 'In me you see the most unfortunate of men, for I have two wives: Wife Number One and Wife Number Two.'

He could have said the same himself.

At the same time he felt that all this suffering was unnecessary, a residue from past ages, nothing to do with love.

# 9

## The Tinkling Key

'One and one make three'

One day Jim was introduced, much against his will, as he didn't want to meet any new faces, to a silent, calm girl, wraith-like in spite of her broad maternal hips; she seemed to him to be dwelling in the shadow of death. Her name was Michèle.

He saw her again. Her company made him forget the conflict between the two others, and he was at peace. She told him her life-story and he told her his; both were eventful, like the lines on their hands. They showed each other photos from their childhood.

She had a bookcase full of old engravings and she went through them with him, describing and explaining.

No, she told him, she wasn't dying of a disease but simply from not having found any incentive to live.

He visited her often.

Three months later, his mother died after a painful illness. He spent the last few weeks at her side.

Right up to the end, his mother's forefinger, lying on the sheet, made a sign meaning 'No' whenever the doctor or the nurse came to give her an injection. She didn't want to have a veil drawn between her and death.

Jim, at his own request, was left sitting alone with his mother's body. He went over their life together. He understood her better.

He re-read a short book of hers, in which she had written about him as a child.

Would he ever have a son himself?

Gilberte came to see him in the morning.

Kate, after lunch.

Michèle, in the evening.

All three were silent, and, in her own way, each was perfect. They all deserved a better man than Jim.

Gilberte was simple in her bearing, and Kate intense.

It seemed to Jim that there was communication between Michèle and his mother. What were they saying to one another?

An intuition flashed through his mind: was it Michèle who was to bear him a son? A son would make her want to stay on earth. Even if she died in bearing him she would die happy. Her strength and her weakness weren't the same as his own, the two wouldn't be added together, they'd cancel each other out; the son would be better than his parents. Gilberte had been too frail. Kate and he destroyed their children in spite of themselves. Would Michèle understand Gilberte?

He resolved to tell Michèle everything and ask her if she'd really like to do it.

He did.

And she said yes.

He must announce the news to Kate, and then to Gilberte.

One morning, when they woke, Jim said to Kate that he had something to tell her, something rather lengthy. The girls and Mathilde were away, Kate and Jim were alone. They settled down in their bed.

Kate knew of Michèle only as Jim's partner in one or two art-dealing matters.

Jim told her carefully the whole story of himself and Michèle, and that they wanted a son, and why.

Kate listened gently till the end, kindly disposed and apparently marvelling, and said:

'What a lovely story, Jim!'

Jim couldn't believe his ears. He had never understood Kate.

She was lying very still. Tears began running down her face.

After a time, in a low voice, she began remonstrating:

'What about me, Jim? What about me, and the children I wanted? Didn't you want them, Jim?'

'Oh, Kate! More than anything!'

Her eyes stung him and stabbed him.

She was like a tortured lamb.

'They'd have been beautiful, Jim!' And she sobbed.

Jim wished he had never been born. He was taking deep, sighing breaths, as Kate sometimes did at night.

'I'm a mother, Jim, a mother before all else.'

Jim thought of her two 'only daughters'. He was going on to bring up their deadly misunderstandings but Kate wasn't listening any longer; she was thinking. Her face was turning pale and her eyes hollow; she was becoming a Gorgon.

Each saw in the other the murderer of their children.

Kate said softly:

'You're going to die, Jim. Give me your revolver. I'm going to kill you, Jim.'

Jim thought of going through with it, just to finish with everything. He'd despise himself if he didn't.

Kate went on demanding the revolver, insistently, like an invalid, astonished by Jim's refusal.

She sat up, looked at him and saw him wavering.

'You're a coward, you're frightened! But the moment's come.'

She realized that Jim wouldn't give in. She bounded out of bed, flew to the front door, locked it and threw the key out of the window. They heard the key tinkle on the stones of the court-yard.

Then she walked towards her desk in which, no doubt, the revolver was kept.

Jim guessed her intention and barred her way. Her whole appearance became frightful; fear took hold of Jim, he was locked in with a mad woman. She advanced on him, attacking him with nails, teeth, everything.

Jim seized her hand but she wrenched it away easily; her fingers at this moment were stronger than his, which she nearly succeeded in twisting.

It would torture him less to resist her blows than her tears. She leapt at him; and, though he hated doing it, he hit her on the chin, just hard enough. She swayed, and he carried her to the bed. When he had swabbed her face with a wet towel she came round and spoke a few words. The crisis of violence was over.

The hours passed heavily. Kate was a convalescent victim and Jim a murderous nurse. They were thinking, but no longer communicated their thoughts. Jim imagined he could see crystals forming in the air.

The door was still locked.

They telephoned from time to time to Kate's Freudian friend, but she was lunching out.

Jim kept a watchful eye on Kate every time she went near the desk.

The confrontation between them lasted till dusk.

At last the friend replied. They asked her to come, pick up the key and open the door.

She did, and they told her what had happened.

'You're a criminal,' she told Jim. 'And you know you agree with me.' Jim raised his eyebrows but didn't answer. 'Kate has kept her head completely. There are various inferences to be drawn from the break between you.'

Neither Kate nor Jim flinched at this. Jim felt that the woman enjoyed saying 'the break' – what business was it of hers, anyway?

'Kate hasn't eaten since yesterday,' the friend went on. 'Will you go out and buy something?'

'Yes,' said Jim. 'But I'd rather take the revolver with me.'

'There's no revolver here,' said Kate.

'Do you swear that's true?' said Jim, astonished.

'I swear.'

Jim ran to the desk, opened it up, pulled out two drawers, found the revolver and put it into his pocket. Kate was upon him already, but he pushed her away. Were they going to fight again? No. Kate gave a smile which meant, 'Who cares? I've got plenty of time . . .'

Jim went out, and came back with food. Was this their last dinner together? They ate in almost complete silence, without hurrying.

Jim took his leave. He always gave Kate a good-bye kiss; would he give her one now?

She kept her face away from him, and they shook hands.

He would wait to hear from her.

## 10

# *The Second Plunge into the River*

Kate sent a wire to Jules: 'Need you. Come.'

Jules was annoyed, and grumbled to himself as he took the train. He was thinking, 'Kate doesn't say why. It must be because of Jim. I wish they'd leave me in peace!'

He went to sleep in the carriage. He saw a big roan horse galloping. A little mare joined it, galloping alongside; first one was in front, then the other. From time to time they stopped and sniffed at one another, and bit and kicked; then off they went again, pounding along furiously, jumping walls which got higher and higher, clearing them with nothing to spare, under a black sky. Exhaustion was making them grow thinner, their coats were long and matted, and there were gleams of fire in the breath spurting from their nostrils.

Jules woke up thinking, 'Jim's accepting Kate's freedom now, just as I've had to accept it for a long, long time – and she'll never forgive him for it. She likes her Paul because he knows what he wants.

'Jim was easy for her to take, but hard to keep. Jim's love drops to zero when Kate's does, and shoots up to a hundred with hers. I never reached their zero or their hundred.

'Why it is that Kate, who's so much in demand, nevertheless makes a gift of her presence to us two? . . . Because we paid complete attention to her, as if she was a queen; because, between

.the two of us, we've been better than anyone else at giving her what people call love.'

He remembered his game of dominoes with Jim, in the train taking them to Lucie. 'What would have happened if Lucie had accepted me? I was a talker, I was proud of my wit. Would Lucie, with her wisdom, have ground me down as much as Kate has?

'How would she have fashioned our marriage? What sort of a pair would we have become?'

Jules pictured himself as an old man, like Lucie's father, walking in the park of the tall white house; and Lucie as an old lady with her arm through his, glancing at him with kindly, observant eyes.

The picture was too beautiful . . .

Next, he imagined Lucie and Jim married, in a big house, and himself there too. They had children. Life flowed onwards surely and gently, everybody worked in calm contentment, they were all conscientious and orderly, even Jim. And everybody loved Jules.

After that he remembered the single night he had spent with Odile, one time when she was on her way through Paris, and everything was over between her and Jim.

It was she who had raped him, Jules, and after a while he had let her do as she liked. He had been wide-eyed and astonished, like a child in front of a Christmas tree, and they had never laughed so much. But one night like that was enough for Odile, and almost for him too. It was a sample, and not meant to be more; he had told Jim about it; and Odile described it to the girls in the café, who winked at him conspiratorially.

Kate, Kate – it was in her that he had encountered reality. And it had broken him to pieces.

★

As soon as Jules arrived Kate consulted him about her professional affairs, and he gave her advice of whose value he was only half-convinced himself. She asked him to telephone Jim and invite him to join them both for a drive that same day, in her open car. She prevented them from getting a chance to talk together on their own.

Jim accepted.

What was the programme to be?

Kate was gambling on the speed of her car and taking almost imperceptible risks.

Jules was sitting in the back, as usual. There was an atmosphere of expectancy, as when they had walked by the lake before the meeting with Harold.

They came to the bank of the Seine, out in the suburbs.

Kate said to Jules:

'If you want to get back to Paris in time for your dinner-appointment, you can take the train from this station, Jules.' She pulled up at a crossroads.

Jules got out and came round to the door. She kissed him gravely.

Then, with eyes shining, she said:

'Watch us carefully, Jules!'

She let in the clutch and bore Jim away. Instead of turning to the right to take the inviting road along the riverside she drove straight on and started across the narrow bridge, which was under repair.

Jim was on the point of asking her, 'Why this way?' But, after all, what did it matter?

Jules watched.

The roadway and the narrow pavements of the bridge were made of freshly tarred planks.

Half-way across, on the left hand side, there was a stretch of thirty yards without a parapet, and beyond that there were men at work.

Kate swerved to the left and her front wheel grazed the edge of the pavement. Jim had a premonition.

She straightened up. The thirty yards would soon be behind them.

She accelerated and put the wheel hard over to the left.

The car jumped on to the pavement, first one wheel, then the other, making for empty space.

Too late to straighten up this time, even if the steering-wheel had been in Jim's hands – and it was in Kate's.

Action was useless. So he might just as well do nothing at all. How cleverly Kate had spread her net! There was no escape. Jim had thought of various possibilities, but not this one.

And she was coming with him!

Ah! So she loved him after all . . . ? Then he loved her!

She turned to him with a mischievous, comradely glance, as if they had plenty of time; as if they were, once more, setting out on a journey of adventure together.

Her glance said: 'You see, Jim, I've won this time.'

The archaic smile had never been so pure.

Kate turned the car over like a wheelbarrow.

A yell from Jules sketched a fiery triangle in the air over their heads.

The seconds were multiplied by a thousand.

Time was transformed, a wonderful leisure extended before them.

The landscape was turning upside down. Jim could feel Kate like a red idol at his side, attracting him like a magnet. He let himself be drawn passively into her splendour. In the darkness he could see, on each side of her, curled up with its legs retracted, a big white spider . . . No, it was moving . . . It was Harold's hands.

## II

## *The Crematorium Furnace*

Jules could sense something coming when Kate said, 'Watch us carefully!' and he had a moment of piercing distress when he noticed the gap in the parapet. Had Kate once more made ready to strike? The first swerve to the left was tentative, but the second wrung a cry from him and the car plunged down towards the water.

Kate hadn't chosen her hour but, even better, even more satisfying for her, her instant.

Jules still hoped wildly to see Jim jumping out and Kate wriggling clear and swimming like an eel. Perhaps it was all just one more trick to frighten him.

The car, inverted, came down covering them both like a lid, making a gigantic splash in the flooded Seine. And nothing came up again.

Jules would never have again the fear that had been with him since the day he met Kate, first that she would deceive him – and then, quite simply, that she would die, for she had now done that too.

Kate and Jim were in the water as in a winding-sheet. Strangely, they were not twined together in an embrace. Indeed, they had died because they had come apart.

The bodies were found entangled in the bushes of a little island which had been submerged by the flood.

Jules accompanied them to the cemetery alone.

What was it he had loved in them? Their extremism, trampling on everything; on Jules, and on themselves. Their *privateering*, Kate had called it.

Why hadn't they had children under his name, since he had no objection?

They had left nothing of themselves behind.

Jules had his daughters.

'What a lot's happened,' he was saying to himself, 'between those two leaps into the Seine! The first, as a warning to me, and to charm Jim. The second, to punish us, and to ring up the curtain on something new.'

In his mind he was seeing Kate as she had been at the start, before she had tasted blood; Kate brilliant and gay, winning races by setting off at 'Two!' Kate generous and irresistible. Kate severe and unconquerable. Kate-Alexander-the-Great, Kate-Rose-of-the-Winds; Kate disarmed for a while by his surrender; and Kate eventually enslaving him, binding him with a thong to her victorious chariot, subjecting him to her triumphal progress.

Kate's flanks, luminous, remote, when he was in the trenches. His first leave, and the bathos of the hero's return.

The emptiness of their marriage, intuitively foreknown by Jim. But, in the beginning, they had shared a tremendous happiness, their children; a happiness which had always eluded Jim's grasp.

In twenty years Jim and he had never quarrelled. Such disagreements as they did have they noted indulgently.

Do lovers ever get on so well together? Jules tried to think of a couple who accepted each other so wholeheartedly as he and Jim.

Jim had taken Lucie and Kate away from him. No. Jules had given them to Jim so as not to lose them, and because they were the best he had to give.

Jim's faith in life was drawn from them; and they in turn drew nourishment from Jim, steadily, calmly, and this gave Jules the leisure for contemplating them.

Kate and Jim had made a religious cult of one another and had risen to exalted heights; but their worship had broken down when it became a matter of day-to-day living.

Had they loved conflict for its own sake? No. But their battles had bewildered Jules, made him dizzy to the point of nausea.

A sense of relief was flooding into him.

The van was drawing up at the crematorium.

Jules made his way into the inner precincts, where the furnace was.

Jim's coffin was even larger than life. Kate's, beside it, was a jewel-case by comparison. Both went up in flames, inch by inch, as they glided into the blinding maw of the furnace.

After an hour the iron trolley came out again. Kate's skeleton, white-hot, suggested even now the outline of her body. She was like a victim emerging triumphant from torture. The skeleton cooled down, falling into dust. A fragment of the skull remained, in a friable state, and was finished off with a silver mallet.

Then it was Jim's turn – Jim the tall, her fellow-victim. There was something left of his skull too.

The ashes were collected into urns and put into a locker, which was then sealed.

Left to himself, Jules would have mingled the ashes.

Kate had always wanted hers to be scattered in the wind on a hilltop.

But that was against the regulations.

*Kate's intimate diaries have been discovered, and will perhaps appear in print.*

# Afterword: Henri-Pierre Roché Revisited

It was in 1955 that I discovered Henri-Pierre Roché's novel, *Jules et Jim*, among other second-hand books on the Stock Bookshop stall in the Place du Palais-Royal.

The book had come out two years earlier, but had passed unnoticed; the critics had been neither favourable nor unfavourable, there had been practically no reviews, as is often the case when the author's name is unknown. What caught my attention was the title: *Jules et Jim*. I was captivated immediately by the resonance of the two Js. Then, turning the book over to read what was on the back of it, I saw that the author, Henri-Pierre Roché, had been born in 1879 and that *Jules et Jim* was his first novel. But then, I thought, this debutant novelist is now seventy-six years old! What can a first novel written by a septuagenarian be like?

From the very first lines, I fell in love with Henri-Pierre Roché's prose. At that time, my favourite writer was Jean Cocteau for his quickfire sentences, their perceptible dryness and the precision of his images. I was discovering, in Henri-Pierre Roché, a writer who seemed to me to be stronger than Cocteau, for he achieved the same kind of poetic prose using a less extensive vocabulary, and making ultra-short sentences from everyday words. Through Roche's style emotion is born out of the void, the emptiness of all the rejected words; it's even born out of ellipsis. Later, on examining Henri-Pierre Roché's manuscript, I saw that his deceptively naïve style resulted from the enormous percentage of words and phrases which had been crossed out; out of a whole page, covered with his round, schoolboy's handwriting, he finally allowed only seven or eight sentences to remain, and even they had had two thirds cut. *Jules et Jim* is a novel about love in telegraphic style, written by a poet who has forced himself to forget his culture and to string words and thoughts together in the way a laconic, down-to-earth peasant would do.

As you might imagine, my enthusiasm for *Jules et Jim* extended to its characters and to their adventures. I lived for the cinema and preferred films to books, watching them at a rate of sixteen or twenty a week. Since I was a film critic on the daily *Arts-Spectacles*, I had the opportunity to fulfil my passion. When I read *Jules et Jim*, I had the feeling that I had before me an example of something the cinema had never managed to achieve: to show two men who love the same woman, in such a way that 'the public' are unable to make an emotional choice between the characters, because they are made to love all three of them equally. It is that element, that anti-selectivity, which struck me most forcibly in this story which the editor presented as 'a triangle of pure love'.

A few months later, watching an American serial film which impressed me, a Western called *The Naked Dawn* by Edgar Ulmer, my thoughts returned to *Jules et Jim*, and in the review I did of the Western, I wrote the following: *One of the most beautiful modern novels I know is* Jules et Jim *by Henri-Pierre Roché, which gives us the lifetime of two friends and their companion in common, who love each other tenderly and with almost no clashes, thanks to a new and aesthetic moral ethic which is constantly under review.* The Naked Dawn *is the first film to give me the impression that a cinematographic* Jules et Jim *is possible.*

The following week, I received this letter: *Dear François Truffaut, I was most impressed by your few words about* Jules et Jim *in* Arts, *particularly 'thanks to a new and aesthetic moral ethic which is constantly under review'. I hope you will find this again, and even more in,* Deux anglaises et le continent, *a copy of which you will be receiving.* Henri-Pierre Roché.

I replied to Henri-Pierre Roché and we kept up quite a regular correspondence for three years until his death. I went to visit him at his house in Meudon two or three times. The train went by the end of his garden. Henri-Pierre Roché was seventy-seven years old at the time. He was very tall and thin, he had the same sweetness as his characters, and was very like Marcel Duchamp, about whom he spoke all the time. He had known Derain, Picabia, le Douanier Rousseau, Max Ernst, Braque (they used to fight each other in the boxing ring), he had been Marie Laurencin's lover, he had introduced Picasso to the Americans, forty years later he discovered Wols, and all his life he had admired Marcel Duchamp, and based the character in his third novel, Victor, on him (this was unfinished, but was published in 1977 by the Georges Pompidou National Centre for Art and Culture).

Let's go back to 1956. In one of my first letters to Roché, I told him that, if ever I got to make films, I would love to make one of *Jules et Jim.* The idea pleased him. We decided that, when the time came, I would set up the construction of the screenplay and he himself would write the dialogue he was planning, according to his own terms, 'well-spaced and tight'. On 23 November 1956 he wrote to me: *Have you read* Mon amant se marie *by Thora Dordel? It is magnificent, but you may not be able to find it. I could lend it to you. In 1915 I and a Russian translated* Uncle Vania *by Chekov. Too early. No one wanted to have anything to do with it then. Idem in about 1906 for* La Ronde *by Schnitzler.*

In December 1957 Henri-Pierre Roché travelled, at about seventy-eight years of age, to come and see my first short film, *Les mistons,* and, spontaneously, he wrote a short essay which he addressed to the paper *Arts,* but which I didn't dare to have printed as I was the cinema critic on that paper! I explained to Henri-Pierre Roché that my desire to make the film of *Jules et Jim* was still as strong as ever but that the whole enterprise seemed to me to be too difficult for a beginner, and that first I would make *Les quatre cents coups*. He understood my point of view, but on 28 December he sent me a letter which the egoism of my twenty-five years prevented me from paying enough attention to: *I shall be happy if I am still around when you attack* Jules et Jim. *I should like to follow you as closely as possible. If you find any reasons or pretexts for us to meet, tell me.*

Believing that I could sense some relationship between Roché's wisdom and the lofty view of Jean Renoir, I sent him an issue of *Cahiers du Cinéma*. In his letter of 18 March 1958, he wrote to me: *Many thanks for your 'Interview with Jean Renoir'. It was a revelation for me. It is so wise, instructive, moving, driving, human, true.* Then he talked about his son Jean-Claude, of whom he was increasingly proud: *My son works in the Camargue. He has had some success and some invitations abroad with his bits of film, in biological circles (Jean Rostand, Jean Painlevé), but also because of the pure beauty, the colours and the relentlessness of his observation (celebration of insects coupling). He would be happy to show them to you.*

When he sent me a signed copy of *Deux anglaises et le continent*, Roché wrote a sentence, which I quote from memory, saying that if this second novel met with no more success than *Jules et Jim* had, he would renounce literature. Nevertheless, on 22 October 1958, he wrote to me: *And all I have to do is to write a third little book, which is becoming quite essential! In fact I've started, and I believe you would like certain of its rhythms, but I haven't yet found the unity of the bias.* This was obviously about the novel which was entitled first *Totor*, then *Victor*, which I mentioned earlier.

Winter 1958–9. I was making *Les quatre cents coups*. Jean-Claude Vrialy had a cameo part and he turned up during a night scene

on the rue du Faubourg Montmartre, and surprised me by bringing with him Jeanne Moreau, whom I had admired in the theatre
in *Cat on a Hot Tin Roof.*

We improvised this little scene, which we made quickly
because of the rain and cold, and, enthused by the actress, I sent
four photos of her to Henri-Pierre Roché, to ask him his opinion.
He replied to me on 3 April 1959: *Dear young friend, your wonderful
letter! . . . Many thanks for the photos of Jeanne Moreau. I like her. I
am happy that she likes Kathe! I hope to meet her some day, yes, come
and see me when you like, I'll wait for you.*

I received that letter on 5 April, and four days later Henri-Pierre
Roché died, very quietly, sitting up in bed, as they were giving
him his daily injection in the forearm.

In 1961 I finally decided to make the film of *Jules et Jim.* The writer
was no longer there to write the 'well-spaced and tight' dialogue,
but Jean Gruault and I made ourselves stay faithful, and more-
over *Jules et Jim* is probably the only 'new wave' film to have such
a full commentary, read as a voice-over, which is drawn almost
entirely from the book.

While the film was being shot and edited, I often found myself
pushing the screenplay to one side and opening my copy of the
novel again, making a note of several splendid phrases to 'preserve
intact' and integrate into the soundtrack of the film. As this essay
is aimed towards making the author of two marvellous novels
better known, I shan't describe the atmosphere of anxiety and
exaltation which surrounded the filming of *Jules et Jim.* I shall
only say that Jeanne Moreau gave me courage every time I was
overcome by doubt. Her qualities as an actress and as a woman
made Kathe – who became Catherine – real before our very eyes,
plausible, crazy, abusive, passionate, but above all adorable, that
is to say worthy of adoration. I had cast the Austrian actor Oskar
Werner to play the role of Jules, and he was admirable. The new

comedian Henri Serre, tall, thin, gentle and honest, was Jim. I had chosen him for his resemblance to Henri-Pierre Roché.

The completed film was released at the beginning of 1962, preceded by the beautiful short film *Vies d'insectes*, about dragon-flies mating, written by Jean-Claude Roché. The success of *Jules et Jim* was instantaneous, and I enjoyed it doubly because the novel, nine years after its first publication, became a bestseller at last and was soon to be translated into English, Spanish and German.

Jeanne Moreau and I both received a considerable number of letters, not only from within France. All over the place, young mothers named their newborn infants Jim, Jules and Catherine. It seems to me, and it's too bad if I'm wrong, that eighteen years after the event I can mention the most important letter of them all, which I received from an old lady called Kathe who had been the true heroine of *Jules et Jim*, the object of that long, shared love of two friends.

*Sitting in that darkened cinema, in dread of disguised resemblances and more or less irritating parallels, I was soon captivated, seized by the magic power, yours and Jeanne Moreau's, to recreate experiences which were lived in blindness. It's no miracle that Henri-Pierre Roché should have known the story of the three of us, keeping very close to the actual sequence of events. But what disposition in you, what affinity could have enlightened you to the point of recreating – in spite of the odd inevitable deviation and compromise – the essential qual-ity of our intimate emotions? On that level, I am your only authentic judge because the other two witnesses are no longer here to tell you 'yes'.*

When he saw the film, Jean Cocteau remembered Henri-Pierre Roché and wrote to me: *I know the author whose book you have made into a film very well. He was the most delicate and noble of souls.*

So I had the approval of the real Catherine, but I found myself thinking most about the real Jim. Henri-Pierre Roché was no

longer there to harvest the fruits of his tree, and that was beginning to torment me. I was convinced that I was too young to
make with the camera what Roché had drawn with his biro. The
exact thing which I had most admired on reading the book was
the fifty years of retirement between the living of the events and
the author's narration of them. What is more, I had some knowledge of that feeling, for in my youth, principally under German
occupation, I had lived through moments of pain and oppression
the memory of which made me smile ten years later. I was less
than thirty years old when I made *Jules et Jim*, and I had forced
myself to make not a *young film* but quite the opposite – an *old
man's film*, and I wasn't sure I'd pulled it off!

When Henri-Pierre Roché died on 9 April 1959, few newspapers
noted his disappearance, and then generally in one or two lines,
for this extraordinary man was not to be a famous one. What is
more, Georges Auric very recently devoted a chapter to him in
his book *Quand j'étais là . . .*, and the chapter is called 'La Vie
obscure de Henri-Pierre Roché'.

His father died when he was very young, and Henri-Pierre
Roché was brought up by his mother with a combination of
passion and strict authority. He went to the School for Political
Sciences, but since painting attracted him more than a career in
administration, he studied drawing at the Académie Julian and
then gave that up because he felt he wasn't talented enough. He
began to collect paintings and translated the Chinese poems
which Georges Auric, Albert Roussel and Fred Barlow set to
music. Roché remained a dilettante all his life, for he always
preferred other's work to his own, and he applied to the letter
the advice that Albert Sorel, his professor at the School for Political Sciences, gave him, which is transcribed, word for word, in
*Jules et Jim*:

Afterword

What would you like to be?

A diplomat.

Do you have a great fortune?

No.

Can you add, with some semblance of legitimacy, a famous or illus-
trious name to your surname?

No.

In that case, give up diplomacy.

But then what shall I become?

An inquiring mind.

That's not a job.

It's not a job yet. It soon will be. The future is for professional inquiring minds. The French have shut themselves away behind their frontiers
for far too long. They should travel. You will always find some newspapers which will pay for your escapades.

It was on a trip to Germany, probably in about 1907, that Roché
met the young Jewish writer Frantz Hessel, made friends with
him, and later made him the Jules of *Jules et Jim* (I don't know the
maiden name or even the nationality of the girl who was to
become Frantz's wife, Helen Hessel, the Kathe of *Jules et Jim*).
Other Germans Roché became friends with or admired, since he
spoke and wrote fluent German, were Peter Altenberg, Keyser-
ling and Arthur Schnitzler.

The fact about Roché which is most often mentioned, and
which is considered, maybe even by him in the first place, to have
been a brilliant move, is that he organized the meeting between
Gertrude Stein and Picasso, probably around 1910. It was during
the same period that he became adviser to and buyer for an
American collector, John Quinn, a collaboration and friendship
which were to last until 1925, when Quinn died.

Roché was declared unfit for service when the army was mobi-
lized in 1914, and he was the victim of an anonymous

denouncement. He was suspected of spying for Germany –
simply because, for several years, he had been receiving important
correspondence from across the Rhine – and was arrested and
put into prison for two weeks. Out of this experience he wrote
his first book, a slim volume of fifty pages which already demon-
strates his lively and joyful style, called: *Deux semaines à la
conciergerie pendant la bataille de la Marne* (Paris, Attinger Frères,
Editeurs, 1916).

But I get the strong impression that it was in Roché's nature
to hide his greatest emotions and that that injustice was not
entirely unconnected to his almost immediate departure for the
United States, thanks to a mission for the French High Commis-
sion in Washington. It was there, in New York, that he met up
again with his friend Marcel Duchamp, who was busy writing
his major work *La mariée mise à nu par ses célibataires, même*.

During that period of the First World War, New York was full
of refugee artists who were revolutionising the artistic atmosphere of the city, and astonishing it with their casualness. Francis
Picabia was one of them, along with his wife, the musician Gabri-
elle Buffet, Edgar Varèse and the extravagant poet-boxer Arthur
Cravan, who was possibly similar to Oscar Wilde, and who myst-
eriously disappeared in Mexico after 1918.

After John Quinn's death, Roché continued to work at discovering and buying paintings, but it was now for a legendary figure,
the Rajah of India, which meant that he made long and frequent
journeys to India. In 1920, under the influence of Jules Laforgue,
whose *Moralités legendaires* he had always admired, Henri-Pierre
Roché published his second book, *Don Juan*, with 'Editions de la
Sirène', where Cocteau published *La noce massacrée* in the same
year. *Don Juan* is presented as a collection of twenty-eight short
tales consisting of variations on the theme of seduction (Don
Juan and the traveller – Don Juan and Denise – Don Juan and the
Baroness etc.). On the day before the book's publication, Roché,

fearful of his mother's hostility, decided to spare her by publishing it under the pseudonym Jean Roc.

The Second World War and the Occupation of France by the German army forced Roché to become wiser. At last he had a married life, and a son, Jean-Claude, and became a teacher of French, drawing, chess and gymnastics in the Drome, for he had bought a house at Dieulefit. It may have been at this time that he started planning *Jules et Jim*, which didn't come out until 1953. After the war Roché published articles on painting and reviews of exhibitions. The glory of Picasso and of Duchamp was at its zenith, and Roché was frequently invited to comment on French painting since the beginning of the century.

What he wrote of his friend Marcel Duchamp could just as easily apply to himself: *his greatest work is the use of his time.* In fact, Henri-Pierre Roché devoted his life to women. In order not to hurt his mother, who adored him, he remained single for a long time. He lived alone but constantly kept three regular mistresses close to body and heart, as well as additional passing, almost daily, conquests. He made a work of art out of his love-life for, from 1905 until his death more than fifty years later, he kept a personal *Diary*. It was the daily and methodical account of his adventures, sometimes written for a few pages in English or German when he wanted to elude the jealousy of such and such a companion of the moment.

After Roché's death, in agreement and in collaboration with his widow, Denise, I had a large part of this *Diary* typed to save it from destruction, but, after two years of typing, the secretary we had employed to do this work chose to abandon it, because she was so disturbed and shocked by what she considered to be 'thoughtless cruelty' in the behaviour of this twentieth-century Don Juan.

Should I have pointed out to this lady-secretary that Henri-Pierre Roché didn't confine to men alone the right to search for the truth, to reinvent love, and that in recent years his character Kathe has become the heroine of the new feminists?

The personal *Diary*, if it were to be published today, would probably fill about twenty volumes, but the French editors I have approached have rejected it because Henri-Pierre Roché, already considered by them to be insufficiently well-known, contrived to give his famous friends, as well as his mistresses, surnames which would make them impossible to identify.

Because of that, the whole enterprise is not considered to be commercially viable, and the *Diary* will remain a secret, but thanks to the splendid novels written in old age about his youth, Henri-Pierre Roché is not a complete unknown.

Of all the portraits we have of him, I particularly like the one made by Jean Paulhan, his friend who undertook to edit *Jules et Jim* at Gallimard: *Yes, he was great, with something languorous about him. He didn't surprise you because he enchanted you. He had a great deal of love for the human race. He thought people were admirable.*

At the end of this long essay, it's time to leave you to ponder Henri-Pierre Roché's sometimes frightening gentleness for yourself. In turn, you will bring him into your life, in turn you will adopt him, in turn, I hope, you will love him.

François Truffaut
Paris, January 1980

Translated by
Katherine C. Foster

*Contemporary ... Provocative ... Outrageous ...*
*Prophetic ... Groundbreaking ... Funny ... Disturbing ...*
*Different ... Moving ... Revolutionary ... Inspiring ...*
*Subversive ... Life-changing ...*

# What makes a modern classic?

At Penguin Classics our mission has always been to make the best
books ever written available to everyone. And that also means
constantly redefining and refreshing exactly what makes a 'classic'.
That's where Modern Classics come in. Since 1961 they have been an
organic, ever-growing and ever-evolving list of books from the last
hundred (or so) years that we believe will continue to be read over and
over again.

They could be books that have inspired political dissent, such as
*Animal Farm*. Some, like *Lolita* or *A Clockwork Orange*, may have
caused shock and outrage. Many have led to great films, from *In Cold
Blood* to *One Flew Over the Cuckoo's Nest*. They have broken down
barriers – whether social, sexual, or, in the case of *Ulysses*, the
boundaries of language itself. And they might – like *Goldfinger* or
*Scoop* – just be pure classic escapism. Whatever the reason, Penguin
Modern Classics continue to inspire, entertain and enlighten millions
of readers everywhere.

'No publisher has had more influence on reading habits than Penguin'
**Independent**

'Penguins provided a crash course in world literature'
**Guardian**

*The best books ever written*

PENGUIN 🐧 CLASSICS

SINCE 1946

Find out more at www.penguinclassics.com